HOME RUN

A BASEBALL GREAT NOVEL

HARPER

An Imprint of HarperCollins*Publishers*

ME
IN
UN

A BASEBALL GREAT NOVEL

TIM GREEN

ALSO BY TIM GREEN

FOOTBALL GENIUS NOVELS

Football Genius
Football Hero
Football Champ
The Big Time
Deep Zone
Perfect Season

BASEBALL GREAT NOVELS

Baseball Great
Rivals
Best of the Best

AND DON'T MISS

Pinch Hit
Force Out
Unstoppable
New Kid
First Team
Kid Owner

Home Run: A Baseball Great Novel

Copyright © 2016 by Tim Green

www.harpercollinschildrens.com

ISBN 978-0-06-231711-7

Typography by Joel Tippie

16 17 18 19 20   CG/RRDH   10 9 8 7 6 5 4 3 2 1

First Edition

For Joe Sindoni, my baseball guru

CHAPTER ONE

PART OF JOSH LOVED his father dearly, but another part...
well, "hate" was a word his mother said you should
never use. He did hate some of the things his father
did. Certainly he hated when his father stood talking
to someone, the way he was right now, when he was
supposed to be coaching baseball. Thankfully, it was
some guy in a suit, not Diane—his dad's girlfriend and
the woman who had destroyed their family—huddled
up with him in the corner of the dugout. But Josh still
stood in the on-deck circle, worried.

Here they were in Baltimore in the championship
game of the final tournament of the season, and his
dad wasn't even paying attention.

He again pushed the image of Diane from his mind.
Instead, he thought of the never-ending stream of

representatives from companies like Nike, Legal Sea Foods, and Marucci Sports—who came to Syracuse and scouted the Titans while his dad piled on the charm. He was always trying to get money for the team. That's who Josh had this guy in the suit pegged for, a rep from some sporting goods company.

"Who else wears a suit to a baseball game?" he silently asked himself.

The crack of a bat turned his attention back to the field.

Benji Lido, one of Josh's two best friends in the world, rumbled down the first-base line, scuffing up puffs of white chalk. The ball rebounded off the left-field wall, but a strong-armed outfielder from Oxford, Mississippi, and too many double cheeseburgers under Benji's sizable belt kept him at first. Their pitcher, Kerry Eschelman, was safely on third. Coach Moose, Josh's dad's muscle-bound assistant, was coaching the Titans' runners at third base. He grinned at Esch and pointed toward Josh in the on-deck circle.

Their catcher, Preston McMillan, gave Josh the high sign.

Benji bounced on the first-base bag, clapping his hands and shouting. "This is *it*, y'all. Heavy hitter two is on the bag! Man in scoring position! And heavy hitter one is about to *blast* it over you rebel boys' heads!"

Josh's teammates elbowed each other and snickered. Even Billy Duncan, their tall, awkward right fielder who'd struck out three times already, broke into a grin from his seat on the end of the bench. Jaden Neidermeyer, Josh's other best friend in the world, was in the dugout keeping stats for the team. Jaden buried her face in her hands, covering her striking yellow-green eyes and honey-brown face. The Oxford Wildcats just stared, still amazed at Benji's loudmouth antics even though they'd gotten a full dose of them now for nearly six whole innings.

Josh swung his bat a final time, then stepped out of the on-deck circle heading for the batter's box. The stands behind the backstop teemed with balloons, banners, caps, and colorful summer clothes. Two parents with their fingers curled around the wire of the backstop talked in the loud, rude voices some adults felt free to use in a kid's world.

"Scoring position? Since when is first base scoring position?"

"Since the LeBlanc kid is up next. Everyone on base is in scoring position when that kid hits."

Josh's cheeks warmed, and he directed his gaze ahead at the catcher and umpire, even though he wanted to turn and enjoy the praise from the well-informed strangers. The Titans were down 3–1, but with Benji on first and Kerry Eschelman on third, everyone knew that Josh could win the game—and the entire tournament—with a home run. He'd already hit one in this game, scoring the only run, and he'd hit eight over the course of the last three days.

With two outs under his belt, Josh knew the Wildcats right-hand pitcher would go for the win himself. His name was Kable Milligan, and he had a fastball that seemed magnetically drawn to the low outside corner of the plate. So while players might be able to get a piece of Milligan's pitches, they rarely ever got a solid hit.

Batting left-handed, Josh took a swing at the first pitch and fouled it off. He glanced at the dugout for his father's encouragement, but the guy in the suit still held his attention. Josh knew that if the sports rep was on the fence about awarding the Syracuse Titans travel baseball team some sponsorship, winning this tournament would go a long way toward the right decision. It was all or nothing.

Despite his father's coaching, Josh hated pressure. He knew true champions got cool under pressure, but he could feel the droplets of sweat beading on his upper lip. And when Benji opened his mouth and began to jaw about heavy hitter one, Josh shot him a look and signaled for total silence.

No such luck.

Benji seemed inspired. "That's *right*! Silent but deadly! That's Josh LeBlanc, ladies and gentlemen! That's heavy hitter one! Over and out, good buddy! We're sendin' some whipped Wildcats down the Mississippi on a riverboat *ride*! Ha! Bring me *home*, my fellow heavy hitter!"

Josh shook his head and bit his lip. He stopped looking at Benji, knowing it had been a mistake to try and shush him. Benji and his mouth were two separate things, and while Benji was lovable and funny, his mouth was like a broken toilet. Getting it to stop running was no easy task.

Josh breathed in deeply the smell of dusty dirt and warm grass, hot dogs and cotton candy. He nodded at the ump and locked eyes with the Mississippi pitcher, a lanky, dark-haired kid with freckles and a mean-looking smile. Milligan wound up. In it came, fast, low, and outside—just as Josh expected.

He stepped toward the plate and barreled up to the ball.

CHAPTER TWO

CRACK.

He could *feel* it. He didn't need to watch.

That ball sailed over the left-field wall.

Josh's team cheered. Benji sashayed around the bases, dancing in front of Josh's slow, steady jog. When Josh crossed home plate and waded through the forest of high fives, he was shocked to see his father hadn't moved from his spot in the corner of the dugout with the stranger. The team was jubilant with a tournament win, but the men were still talking intently.

"Dad?" Josh stood at the entrance to the dugout, looking down and in. Jaden was finishing up the stats. She smiled, giving him a silent thumbs-up for his big home run. But he was unable to return her smile.

"Dad?" he said again. "Is everything okay?"

Josh's father looked up as if waking from a dream. His eyes focused on Josh, and his smile appeared as he nodded his head. "Better than okay, Josh! Nice hit! Great tournament!"

The words suggested everything was fine, but Josh knew his father, his expressions, and his voice well enough to know that something had happened.

In fact, Josh was certain that everything in their lives was about to change.

CHAPTER THREE

AS JOSH HEADED TOWARD his dad, Jaden leaned back to let him pass. She was watching without comment, but her green catlike eyes caught his and froze the moment in time. She had her frizzy hair pulled back in a ponytail. Her straight and narrow nose and the long, dark eyelashes reminded him of the picture in his social studies book of an Egyptian princess.

"Josh?" His father's voice broke the spell. "Come here. There's someone I want you to meet."

His father turned to the stranger. "Josh, this is Jeff Enslinger, the athletic director at Crosby College. . . . It's in Florida. Not far from Orlando."

Mr. Enslinger extended a hand, and Josh took it. "Nice to meet you, Josh."

"Like, Disney World?" It was the only thing that came to Josh's mind.

The AD was nearly as tall as Josh's father but not as thick. He had a weak chin but strong, blue eyes perched above a big, triangular nose. His hair was a blaze of orange spikes. Was he trying to look like a Florida orange?

Mr. Enslinger studied Josh before smiling. "We're about an hour from Disney, but a lot of our students end up working there. There's a whole city underneath that place. You'd be surprised."

"I'd like to go sometime," Josh said.

Mr. Enslinger cleared his throat and gave Josh's dad a questioning look. "Everybody loves Disney."

Josh's dad laughed and thumped Josh's back. "Mr. Enslinger has offered me a job, buddy."

"At Disney?" Josh rumpled his brow.

His father laughed some more, and Mr. Enslinger joined in.

"At Crosby College," his father said. "They've got a Division Three baseball program."

"Which will become Division One in two years," Mr. Enslinger said. "Under your father's direction . . . if he accepts my offer. We're putting a lot of money into it. We've got a deal with Nike to buy all their equipment, and they were the ones who said I should take a look at your dad. He does nothing but win, right? That's

9

how they described him."

Josh had no idea what to say. Out on the field, the two teams were forming lines to shake hands, baseball players caught up in one of the great traditions of the game. He nodded toward his teammates. "Should we shake hands?"

His father glanced at the field. "For sure! Sorry, Jeff, I'll be right back."

"Of course." Mr. Enslinger gave a short nod suggesting sportsmanship was a welcome quality at Crosby College.

Josh hurried out of the dugout, the joy of the big victory already swallowed up by the tar pit of worry. He looked back and watched his father say something else to Mr. Enslinger, then shake hands before jogging onto the field to join his team. Josh pasted a smile on his face, slapped hands, and mumbled, "Good game good game good game," like some caveman chant as he worked his way through the Wildcats' team roster.

His mind spun with questions, none of them comforting. Where would they live? How would they get down there? What school would he go to? What about his friends? Was there a team he could play for in Florida? Who would coach that team? But most of all Josh worried about his mom. Where did she fit into all this?

And would she even join them?

CHAPTER FOUR

JOSH COULDN'T HELP WONDERING if he might be able to stop the whole thing, alter the course of his and his family's lives that very day. Josh wasn't a kid anymore; he was a young man. That's what his mom called him when she was mad, wasn't it? A young man could make decisions and have an impact on the world around him, right?

It might be possible if he played it right.

Never able to make it to the major leagues, his dad talked all the time about Josh's baseball career. It was as if Josh's life was his father's second chance. A first-round draft pick out of high school, Josh's dad spent years in the minor and independent leagues before his retirement—forced on him, if Josh was honest. Where his father had failed, Josh would surely succeed. It was at the heart of their relationship. They spent nearly no time together that wasn't on a ball field or at the batting cage, honing his skills. So, if Josh dug his heels in, he just might be able to unravel the whole college thing. . . .

The hint of tears in the corners of the Mississippi pitcher's eyes jarred Josh back into the present moment. Suddenly the slap of hands and the sun blinking down on them both became monumentally important. This game—and this tournament—meant so much to the players in it because each victory was another rung in the ladder toward the majors. That's what his father had taught him. While Benji would jeer if he saw Kable Milligan's tears, Josh felt a bond of brotherhood.

Each star performance gave you a leg up on the other guys. There were thousands—no, hundreds of thousands—of "other" guys. And fewer than four hundred spots in the show for position players like Josh. He knew that from his dad's career. His dad *never* played a game in the majors. He never even got a September call-up to ride the bench and wear a big-league uniform. It was more than tough, so he understood the Mississippi pitcher's feelings immediately. Between the two of them, Josh had won the day . . . and the trophy.

"Hey." Josh stopped and took hold of the boy's shoulder. "You're one of the best pitchers I've seen. You own that outside corner."

Milligan looked at the ground and muttered, "Thanks."

Josh watched the pitcher trudge past the dugout to be greeted by what had to be his mom and dad. They both draped their arms over Milligan's shoulders as well as each other's in one big group hug.

Josh sighed. Losing stunk, but he knew he'd trade places with Kable Milligan a million times over to have his mom and dad back together. He'd give up even his own dreams to become a major-league player if only things could be the way they were before his dad stopped playing, got Diane as a girlfriend, and moved out of the house. Losing a baseball game—even a big one—didn't compare to losing your family.

And now his dad was thinking about breaking things up even more.

Benji's meaty hand gripped Josh's neck and spun him around. "Kisses for the superstar."

Benji planted a sloppy kiss on Josh's cheek.

"Aww." Josh wiped the slobber from his face as they migrated back toward their own dugout. "That's disgusting, Lido."

Benji gave him a disappointed look. "Heavy hitters have a special bond. It goes beyond a handshake."

"Couldn't you just hug me or something?"

Benji shook his head and sighed. "Sometimes I wonder why I even try to teach you the ways of the world.

Hey, take it easy, heavy hitter. It's not that serious. Why the sad-sack look? You look worse than Duncan, and he hit nothing but air today."

Josh shook his head. He felt like crying himself. "Everything's different. That's all."

"Dude, we won a monster tournament. Look at those hunks of metal." Benji pointed toward the table of trophies the tournament organizers had lined up near home plate. "You and I are gliding into fall ball like a couple of major leaguers. Next stop, the show!"

Benji nodded at his own wisdom.

"So you're going to Major League Baseball, Mr. MLB?" Jaden appeared, eyebrows raised and snapping her stats book shut for the day. "Did you get hit by a pitch, Lido?"

Benji shooed Jaden away with a fluttering hand before holding out his palm to signal *Stop!* like a traffic cop. "Talk to the hand. The people don't want your grumpy and negative opinions. I need to receive my trophy now. Please make way for the heavy hitters."

"You guys just turned thirteen." Jaden looked around the hand and scowled. "The majors are a long way away. You don't even shave."

"What's a beard got to do with it?" Benji was insulted.

"You're the Red Sox fan, Lido." Jaden wore the confident look of a superior mind, and Josh knew she was referring to the raggedy beards the Boston players had worn during the 2013 worst-to-first championship season.

Benji was quick to reply. "You think you're so smart. Too bad you're a Yankees fan *and* a girl. I'm not sure which is worse."

Josh rolled his eyes. "Haven't you learned not to go there, Benji?"

It was too late. Jaden had that fire in her eyes. "Since it took a female to bring you into the world, I can see why you're so down on women."

"Hey, that's my mom you're talking about!" Benji put up his fists like he was entering a boxing ring. Josh grabbed him.

"Let me at her!" Benji struggled.

"If she knocks your lights out in front of all the guys, you'll never live it down, Benji," Josh said.

"I'm not afraid of that karate stuff! Fufitsu or jujitsu or poop-it-sue or whatever it is! Let me at her!"

Josh's dad stepped into their midst. "Benji, cut it."

Crazy about Josh's father, Benji quickly fell into line.

"Let's get the trophies, you guys, and then we need to get this show on the road."

Sensing his dad's impatience, Josh's stomach turned. His dad acted like the huge victory was nothing more than the small and annoying bite of a bug. In fact, his father tapped his foot impatiently as the presenter bragged about the tournament's sixty-seven-year history.

But he was all smiles when he raised the four-foot-high trophy above his head before setting it on the grass. He took the microphone from the presenter and gave thanks to everyone involved in the tournament and the ceremony. He praised the sponsors, then the players on both teams and said they were all wonderful kids. He ended with a big finish.

"This has been a fantastic tournament! Thank you. Thank you all!" Josh's father handed the mic back to the presenter and walked away, leaving people in the stands cheering as the team followed him, laughing and backslapping all the way into the dugout to gather their gear.

"Guys," Josh's dad said after they were settled on the bus back to Syracuse. "This was my last game as your coach, and it was great to go out on a win. I'll never forget it."

The mouths of Josh's teammates dropped open all at once.

Coach Moose looked like he already knew what was happening, and he popped up from his seat and gave Josh's dad a hearty handshake.

"I've taken a job at Crosby College in the sunshine baseball state of Florida," Josh's dad said. He rubbed the younger coach's bristly crew cut with affection. "And don't worry. Coach Moose would never leave Syracuse.

He'll be here with you guys for fall ball, and he'll help with the transition."

His father scratched his neck and gave one of his smiles. "You've been an outstanding team, and I know you'll do great this fall."

Josh blinked as if he'd been slapped, and he didn't care that everyone could hear him speak. "But Dad . . . he offered it to you, like, five minutes ago. You . . . you can't take it just like that. Without . . . like, thinking."

"But, son," his dad said, "I already did."

CHAPTER FIVE

JOSH HUDDLED IN THE backseat of the bus with Jaden and Benji. His mind spun like his little sister twirling fast on the back lawn until she fell in a heap. He just couldn't believe his father would simply move, and to Florida. How far away was that? A thousand miles? More. He grabbed his head and banged it softly into the seat in front of him.

The big machine grumbled and vibrated as it ate up the road. Syracuse, New York, where they lived, was about six hours from Baltimore. The tinted windows and constant bus sounds hypnotized their brains into the lie that they were not even moving. No one paid attention to the darkening trees whisking past. Benji rustled a huge bag of Doritos, slamming chips down by the fistful and crunching, his jaw swinging like a lantern in the wind.

Josh leaned forward and kept his voice low, despite there being no way his dad could hear them from his seat in the front, even if he hadn't been napping. "I mean, I can't believe he's even serious. I had no idea."

"I wonder who's going to coach the team." Jaden had her mother's worry beads out. She'd recently found them in an old box her father had tucked away when they'd moved up from Texas after her mom died. Now Jaden was kneading them with her slim fingers. She said they kept her calm.

"It doesn't even make sense," Benji said through a messy mouthful of chips. "And I'm not saying it to be mean, but really? Crosby College? Who ever heard of that? And did you see that athletic director? Like a clown or something with that orange spiked hair?"

Jaden shook her head. "You can't judge a book by its cover."

"Well, I do." Benji stuck a dusty orange thumb in his own chest. "I don't like the cover, I am *not* reading that book. Don't wag your eyes at me, either. I heard this story on *Entertainment Tonight* that said the most important thing for book sales is the cover."

"Is that where we're getting our news now?" Jaden asked. "*Entertainment Tonight*? Seriously, Lido."

"You two stop already," Josh said. "Come on. My dad

has lost his mind for real this time, and you two are talking about a stupid TV program."

"You're siding with her? My dad loves *ET*, and you're calling it stupid? You might as well be calling my dad stupid, and I know you're not doin' that cuz he'll bring the pain like a dentist's drill." Benji swelled his chest like a hot-air balloon.

Benji took a lot of pride in his dad, a giant of a man who wreaked havoc in the local semipro football league. Even though his real job was in an appliance factory, Benji relished calling his dad a football player.

Josh shuddered. "Just . . . just stop it. Both of you! This could be the end for me."

Benji's hand froze in the bag of Doritos, and he rumpled his brow. "Are you sick?"

"If I move to Florida, I won't see you guys. It's over," Josh said.

Benji looked stunned. "Well . . . you can't. I mean . . . heavy hitters. It's a dynamic-duo thing. It's not all about me. Dude, you're the bomb. I'd be like birthday cake without the ice cream."

Jaden's beads sagged in her hand. She chewed on a knuckle but said nothing.

"Maybe they'll let you stay if you tell them you gotta win that house," Benji said.

"House? What house?" Josh asked. "What are you talking about, Lido?"

"That Home Run Derby," Benji said. "You didn't hear

about it? My dad was talking. First you gotta qualify. You've gotta be on a Youth Baseball Elite League team—which the Titans already are—and you gotta hit twenty home runs during fall ball to qualify for the derby. It's down in Houston in late October. Anyone in YBEL can win. They put a bathtub twenty feet behind the center-field fence. If you qualify and get down there, all you have to do is dump a home run into the tub during the derby and you win a *new house*."

"You're kidding," Josh said.

"Nope." Benji wagged his head proudly. "This Qwik-E-Builders—the sponsors—sell modular homes. Twenty long balls and you're in. For you? You could win that thing easy."

"It's not easy, Lido," Jaden said. "It's like one of those scams they have at golf tournaments where you can win a free car if you get a hole in one. No one ever wins those things."

"It's a *promotion*, Miss Smarty-Pants. It's legit. The FTC regulates these things. My mom said so when my dad got in her face about a sweepstakes she entered. Yeah, the FTC, that's the Federal Trade Commission. You're not the only brains around this joint, sorry to tell you. There's no reason Josh can't win."

Josh huffed. "My dad's not staying here so I can *maybe* win a house. The last thing my dad cares about is a new home. He wouldn't give a nickel for the home we've already got. Stuff is breaking all the time."

They rode for a few more minutes, each of them thinking.

"Wait!" Benji waved a hand in the air, then lovingly folded his arms around the Doritos bag and leaned back in the seat, beaming at them. "I got it!"

"This better not be some other kind of bone-headed contest with a million-to-one odds." Jaden looked at him sharply. "This is serious. Josh could be leaving."

Benji held up a finger, scowling. "I do not mess around about something as serious as cake and ice cream. You know that."

Josh felt a ray of hope.

It was obvious by the rare, thoughtful look on Benji's face that he had the answer Josh needed.

CHAPTER SIX

"YOU RUN AWAY." BENJI stared at them, confident.

"Aw, jeez, Benji," Josh said. "I'm not some little kid with a blanket and an Elmo doll in his lunch box."

Josh looked at Jaden, expecting her to launch an attack on Benji. He got confused when she merely raised an eyebrow.

"Not you too?" he asked.

"Listen, I'm serious," Benji said. "My older brother ran away once, and he was *fourteen*. Whew. You should've seen the action around my house for those three days."

Jaden wasn't whipping Benji with words, so Josh asked, "What happened?"

Benji licked Doritos dust from his lips and looked

around to see if anyone else was listening, then he lowered his voice. "He went camping. Took our pup tent and a couple boxes of cereal. Three days in the woods. Said he needed to find himself. He really did it because my dad was talking about going to Alaska. Had a job on a fishing boat. Wanted to use the money he'd make to race monster trucks. That and the NFL were his childhood dreams, and the NFL . . . . well, you know about his knees. My mom called it a midlife crisis, whatever the heck *that* is."

Benji reached into his bag for a chip. "Anyway, my brother dis*appears*. They call the cops. People are thinking the worst. It's on the news. Crackpots come out of the woodwork. One guy says he saw my brother get on board an alien spaceship. A crazy lady in a turban says he's locked inside a car trunk somewhere, and she can hear him calling for help.

"My mom's going out of her gourd. Now, I barely remember this because I was, like, five, but my dad? Forget Alaska! He and my mom almost got back to*gether*."

Benji's words hung in the air like a genie from Aladdin's lamp, waiting to grant Josh the wish of a lifetime.

Josh swallowed. "They did?"

"Well, yeah, but then my dad ate a pie and it all fell apart." Benji frowned. "That's according to my brother anyway."

"Do we even want to know?" Jaden twisted up her lips.

Benji huffed and popped another bunch of chips into his mouth, talking through a flurry of crumbs. "Well, my mom made a pie. It was for my grandmother's birthday, and he ate it. All of it."

Josh could tell Benji had a story. "Your mom didn't get back together with your dad because he ate your grandmother's pie?"

"Well, I think she would have forgiven him for that, but then he got sick and puked it all up on her wedding dress, and she said that's what you get for eating a whole pie anyway."

"Wait a minute," Josh said. "What are you talking about? Why would your mom's wedding dress be out? They were already married. You said your brother was fourteen."

Benji swallowed. "Yeah. So, he's getting ready for bed and he starts to get sick, gagging and all that, knows he's gonna blow chunks, but my mom's in the bathroom with the door locked, and he *tells* her he's gonna be sick. She shouts at him through the door that she can't open it and for him to just take his fat, pie-eating butt outside to hurl. He can't make it down the stairs—or so he said—and he's trying to open the window to puke out, but he can't get it open because she painted without taping the seams while he was living on his own and

25

so he grabs a box from the closet, first box he sees, and just heaves and . . ."

Benji's head swayed with monumental disappointment. "Her wedding dress was in it. Why, we'll never know."

"A lot of women store their wedding dresses in a box." Jaden piped up. "You can't just *hang* them."

"Of course not." Benji rolled his eyes and rattled the Doritos bag as he dug his fist in. Josh knew he was restraining himself.

Josh held his hand out for a chip. "My parents would think I went crazy, and I don't have a pup tent. I was already thinking about saying I won't go with him . . . to Florida, but who's gonna coach me? I *gotta* make it to the majors. Jaden, you can't be serious about this running-away thing, can you?"

Jaden closed her eyes and shook her head. "Yes and no. Not a pup tent, but you *tell* them you're running away. You tell them you can't live like this anymore. I mean, maybe you disappear for a day. Hide out in my basement or something."

"My basement is better than yours," Benji said, handing Josh another chip and offering the bag to Jaden. "I got an Xbox down there."

Jaden shook her head at the bag and turned to Josh. "Yeah, but my dad's out of town overnight, and I can play dumb and no one gets in trouble. At night Josh can even sleep in his room."

"He lets you stay alone?" Benji couldn't believe it.

Jaden shrugged. "I'm thirteen. He knows I can take care of myself. Plus, my neighbor across the street checks up on me every now and then."

Benji shook his head with disapproval. "Dude, there's been all those break-ins. Druggies from Bricktown. One old man over on Lamont Street got busted up bad last week. Kids stole his TV and some money. Didn't you hear about that?"

Jaden continued as if Benji hadn't interrupted her. "It's the mental thing that'll get your parents. You might have to go to counseling or something, but that's okay. That could keep your dad from leaving. Reevaluate things, just like Benji's dad did."

Benji looked sadly at a chip. "Until the pie."

"Until the pie, yes." Jaden nodded.

Josh munched his chip, and they sat there in silence for a minute before he swallowed and spoke. "My dad would kill me if I ran away. My mom would freak out."

Benji nodded. "Which could actually bring them back together. A common enemy. Like Churchill and Stalin uniting against Hitler, bitter enemies became allies to save the world."

"Hitler?" Josh knew Benji was still trying to get some mileage from the A he got on the World War II essay he'd written on their history final back at the end of the last school year. A week hadn't gone by without him bringing up Winston Churchill, Roosevelt, Stalin, or Hitler so he could remind them about his expertise on the subject.

"Well, not you," Benji said. "But your mental condition. That'd be the common enemy. Your twisted runaway brain is like Hitler, who had a total twisted runaway brain."

Jaden dismissed Benji with the wave of her hand, then said, "Your dad got all those sponsorships for the Titans, Josh. Things are going well here. Look at the tournament you just won. A college job *sounds* good, but college coaches these days sometimes only last a year or two before they get fired, and the money can't be all that great."

"It's so . . . desperate. Crazy," Josh said.

"Exactly, dude." Benji pointed a chip at him. "And desperate times require desperate measures."

"And if I say yes to this plan?" Josh asked. "When would I so-called 'run away'?"

Benji and Jaden looked at each other before speaking at the same time:

"Tonight."

CHAPTER SEVEN

A FEW HOURS LATER they were in New York, making good headway, when the rain began to fall. By Binghamton it was a downpour. With about an hour left to Syracuse, they made their plan and helped Josh come up with the note he would leave for his parents to find, a note that would make them realize what they'd done.

Mom & Dad—
Our family is ruined.
My life is ruined and I can't do this anymore.
I'm leaving to find a better place.

As the bus pulled into the school parking lot where parents waited inside their wet cars, Josh examined the words written in his own solid hand for the fiftieth time. "I don't know, guys. It sounds pretty desperate. I mean, 'a better place'? That sounds like I'm gonna jump off a bridge or something."

"Exactly!" Benji smacked the note with the back of his fingers. "You gotta put that kind of fear into their hearts if you want to have an impact. No sense doing it halfway."

"What do you think?" Josh asked Jaden.

"I think it scares me that I am so much in agreement with this thing," she said, pointing to Benji.

Benji nodded wisely and slurped the last bit of a strand of a red licorice string into his mouth like a lizard's tongue. "It's true. Great minds do think alike."

They parted on the steps of the bus and ran to their respective cars in the downpour. Josh got into the new red Camaro and rode beside his father in silence. Tires hissed through the puddles, and windshield wipers squeaked out their steady rhythm. When his father missed the turn to their house, all he said was "Gotta get gas."

The silence resumed. Josh waited without a word while his father filled the tank under the fluorescent lights of the overhang. After a thump and a click, his father replaced the nozzle and climbed back in.

On the way home from the gas station they had to pass a bad part of the city. Josh wasn't sure about the real name of the six blocks cramped with three-story brick buildings, but Bricktown was what everyone on the north side of Syracuse called it. Beneath a broken streetlight, a handful of young men stood around an oil drum, burning something that smelled awful. Josh saw the glint of bottles flash from beneath their jackets as they raised them to take long swigs.

Just before their car reached the corner, one of the men staggered out into the street, and Josh's father swerved crazily, blaring his horn. Josh's heart galloped, and he turned in his seat to see the man holding up his middle finger, yelling.

"Idiot!" Josh's dad glanced in the mirror but kept going. "You stay away from that place, right?"

"Of course." Josh turned to face front. "I never go there."

"Good," his father said. "I don't even want you walking down that street."

Josh poked his fingers into his pants pocket, toying nervously with the edge of the running-away note he'd written until they stopped in the driveway of the house where they had all once lived together. It was a narrow red house jammed between its neighbors, with a tall, sagging roof. It needed paint and it needed repair.

There they sat, his father thinking and Josh waiting. Silence was no stranger to Josh and his father. It didn't mean anything was wrong. So when his dad patted Josh's leg and spoke, Josh wasn't totally surprised that his father sounded upbeat. "Great win today, on and off the field, right?"

"What do you mean 'off the field'?" Josh asked.

The wipers swiped the windshield, and Josh's house appeared and disappeared, appeared and disappeared, as fresh raindrops spattered the image.

His father looked surprised. "Josh, a Division One coach? I could end up coaching in the Bigs one day if Colby wins a few titles. And you *know* how great it would be to suit up as a Yankee?"

Anger caught flame inside Josh. "I thought you always said that family is more important than anything."

"I did." His father gripped the wheel and turned his whole body toward Josh. "I do. This can help our family, Josh. It can help me *and* you. Your mom and sister too. Do you have any idea how much money major-league coaches make?"

"Probably a lot." Josh moved to reach for the door handle.

"Definitely a lot." His father took hold of Josh's arm to prevent him from getting out. His hand swallowed Josh's arm. It was a hand Josh had seen crush soup cans like tissue paper, and it got his attention now.

"Hey, what's up with you?" his father asked.

Josh looked at his father's dark eyes, tucked beneath the brim of the Titans baseball cap but still glinting in the light of the dashboard. Rain pattered on the roof and hood.

"Our family is broken, Dad. A college job won't fix that."

His father paused and loosened his grip. "Families come in a lot of different shapes and sizes, Josh. It doesn't mean we're not a family. Look at Benji. Look at Jaden."

"Jaden's mother *died*." Josh knew he sounded mean, but he didn't care.

"That's not what I meant," his father said.

"Can you see Mom moving to Florida?" Josh asked.

"Maybe. Why not? She loves the sun."

Josh just shook his head.

His father put the car into park and shut off the engine.

"Come on," he said, getting out of the car.

"Where are we going?" Josh got out too.

His father marched toward the side door that opened into the kitchen, tall and straight as if it wasn't raining at all. He stopped with his fingers on the handle of the battered screen door. "Let's ask her."

"Ask who? Ask what?" Josh said.

"Your mother," his father said. "Let's ask her if she'll move to Florida with us."

The word "us" pierced Josh's heart like an arrow.

CHAPTER EIGHT

JOSH'S FATHER DUCKED HIS head as he marched in, tracking puddles across the kitchen floor. Josh followed and could hear the TV around the corner in the den. Still dripping, Josh hung his equipment bag from one of the coat hooks on the wall leading down into the basement, then shucked off his cleats.

"Laura?" his father's voice boomed through the tiny house.

Josh's mom didn't appear, but his baby sister did. "Dada! Dada! Dada!"

She shrieked, trundled across the floor, and threw herself into their father's arms. He scooped her up like a towel and flung her around. Their laughter filled the kitchen like a million bubbles, bright and clean and bursting with joy.

His father held her high and began dipping her head until they touched noses, their voices like music.

"I'm gonna get you!"

"Hee hee!"

"I'm gonna get you!"

"Hee hee!"

And so they went like the refrain from a song on the radio until Josh's mother appeared in the doorway from the living room. His mom was tall, and she stood at her full height with her arms folded. The look on her face cast a shadow on the kitchen and all its festivities.

"Gary." She gave him a severe nod and reached for a stack of papers on the countertop next to the toaster.

Josh's dad gently set Josh's sister down on the floor, where she began to fuss and whine, bouncing up and down, asking for more.

"Laura," his father said. "We need to talk."

"What are *these*?" She jabbed the papers at him like a knife fighter. "Do you mind telling me? Are we in trouble here?"

His father snatched them without more than a glance and stuffed them into his back pocket. "We're fine. I've got it all covered."

"You do? Look at the yellow one, Gary. It says something about *foreclosure*." His mom put her hands on her hips.

His father waved a thick hand in the air, dismissing

the papers. "Banks like to talk tough. I'll handle them. I've got a plan. They always give you time when you've got a plan."

Josh could see from his mom's pinched face that she wasn't finished. "And the electrician keeps calling. He wants to get paid."

The severity of Josh's mother's voice froze little Laurel in her tracks, and she stumbled over to their mother, clinging to her legs and mewling like a kitten.

His father gritted his teeth, and Josh felt all his newborn hopes and dreams melting away.

"Guys." Josh stepped between them. "Stop. Mom, Dad has some really great news. Right, Dad?"

His father's face softened a bit, and he put a hand on Josh's head. "Can we sit down?"

"Of course." His mother was still stiff, but she scooped up Laurel and marched back through the small front room they called their living room even though it looked out onto the back lawn and into the even smaller room they called a den, home to the TV and a couch that some might call a love seat since three was a crowd. In the corner sat his father's La-Z-Boy, its fake brown leather worn pale and nearly through on the arms and headrest. It had been an empty reminder of his father's absence these past several months, but now his father took his throne as if he'd never left.

His father told the story of Crosby College, revealing details Josh hadn't known. Jeff Enslinger, the school's athletic director, had been talking to him for a month. His father said he'd visited Crosby during the Titans' Sunshine Tournament in Tampa three weeks ago and seen the great work being done to the facilities. Josh replayed their three days in Tampa, wondering when in the world that had happened until he came up with an afternoon when Coach Moose had taken the team to Busch Gardens. Josh had been so excited, he barely noticed that his father had stayed behind.

His father stopped talking and looked pointedly at Josh before he continued. "It's the best thing for Josh too. I can keep coaching him. Keep an eye on him anyway. People will want to do right by him if they know his dad is in charge of the college baseball program. That's how it works, especially when we go Division One."

Josh's mother didn't seem impressed by any of it, but Josh knew she'd been struggling lately. It wasn't uncommon for him to hear her through the locked door of her bedroom crying.

"So," Josh's father continued, "I was thinking . . . maybe you could come down there too. We could all go. Leave this house. Get out of these crazy winters."

Josh looked at his mom. Her eyes widened with surprise. This was everything Josh had been dreaming of, hoping for, praying for. Finally, their family could be back together. He didn't care if they lived on the moon or in the middle of the Mohave Desert. If the four of them could be together, Josh would go anywhere.

Josh's mother blushed.

She opened her mouth to speak, and he held his breath because he had no idea what she might say.

CHAPTER NINE

"I HADN'T EVEN THOUGHT about getting back together, Gary." His mom's voice was soft, but scratchy with feeling. "I didn't think that was on the table."

Josh felt sorry for his mom. She reminded him of an autumn maple leaf, trembling in the wind, beautiful but ready to fall.

His father cleared his throat and shook his head. "I'm sorry. That's not what I meant. Um, I meant we could all move down. I don't see us getting back together. That's not really part of this. I'm just trying to keep us close—as a family."

The color drained from his mother's face in an instant. Josh's heart dropped to his feet.

"Get out." His mother pointed toward the door, her voice still soft, but terrible now.

Josh's father stood. "I just think—"

"Get out." She raised her voice to a normal level, not looking at Josh's father, but still her quavering finger pointed at the door.

"It's not fair to make him have to choose." Josh's father backed away, scowling.

"Get out!" She jumped to her feet and screamed. "I said, get out!"

Laurel's face crumpled. She took three big gasps of air. Josh plugged his ears just as she began a piercing howl. His father stormed out. The kitchen door crashed shut. Josh shook his head, grabbed his baseball and glove, ran up the stairs, and slammed the door behind him as well. He dove onto the bed and buried his head in the pillows, pressing them tight to his face and screaming.

"I hate you! I hate you *all*!"

CHAPTER TEN

AFTER THINGS FINALLY QUIETED down, Josh heard his mom carry Laurel up the stairs and put her to bed. His mom knocked softly on his door, saying his name. Josh refused to answer. He loved his mother and he felt sorry for her, but hadn't she had a hand in all this? He could easily recall her nagging his father over and over about money, money, money. She'd done it tonight, hadn't she? The stupid electrician's bill? He'd heard them fighting beneath his bedroom for years on end, and a part of him understood why his father had called it quits.

So he bit his lip and remained silent until she gave his door one final, shocking thump, spit out the word "fine," and went away. She slammed her door too, and Josh bolted upright, banging his head on the low, slanted ceiling above his bed.

"Ow! Stupid ceiling! Stupid, crummy bedroom!" He slithered off the bed, grabbed a duffel bag, and began stuffing it with some clothes. The idea of running away didn't seem like a plan anymore; it seemed like a necessity. It didn't seem like a way to get his parents back together; it seemed like a way for him to get away from them both. He grabbed his Speed Hitter, thinking he'd need the training bat to stay sharp. On the edge of his mind flickered the worry about where he'd ultimately end up living and how he'd care for himself, but the cloud of anger and determination was too thick for him to think about that. He put a ball in the pocket of his glove and duct-taped it closed, adding it to the duffel bag.

He texted Benji, then Jaden, letting them know that their plan was in full swing.

With his own heavy breathing the only sound to be heard through the house, he crept down the stairs ninja-like in his socks, planting his feet heel to toe with the care of a watchmaker. He removed the note from his pocket and set it on the table.

At the kitchen door, he threw on his sneakers and grabbed a raincoat off its hook before letting himself out into the dark, dreary night. Outside, cold gusts of wind whipped his face with rain. Energy from the weather rushed through his body, filling him with excitement. He slung the bag across his back, gripped his Speed Hitter, and took off at a lope up the street.

Before rounding the corner, he took a final glance at his house. He snorted at its gloom and kept going in the misty glow of the streetlamps. The roads were wet and wild and empty, but Jaden was waiting for him at the door to her house. She swung it open as he climbed the steps onto the covered front porch. Wind rushed in as he dumped the dripping duffel bag and training bat on the floor.

"You're all wet." She used her shoulder to close the door, then helped him out of his coat and hung it on a rack inside the door. "We can let it dry for a few minutes, but let's not forget to bring it to the basement. I'm sure someone will be coming to my door tomorrow looking for you, and it'd be pretty dumb if your coat was hanging here. Sneakers too."

Josh already had his sneakers off and in the rubber tray where Jaden's sneakers rested beside a pair of her father's running shoes. He pointed to his stuff. "What about this?"

"Downstairs, I think." She motioned to him and opened a door he hadn't even realized was there beneath the staircase leading to the second floor. "It's not bad, and no one can see in."

He followed her into the stuffy, gloomy space, blocked off from the really nasty part of the basement by some paneled walls that bowed in and out. On the floor was a carpet so thin it might have been painted onto the concrete. In the corner sat a dusty old tube TV with a coat hanger for its antenna. A musty plaid couch backed into one wall. It faced a large chrome-and-glass-framed copy of Vincent van Gogh's *Starry Night* on the opposite wall.

"My dad calls this his think tank. One small window over there. Not much sound. His favorite painting. Perfect place to hide. Just no Xbox." She pointed at the sad-looking TV.

Josh flicked the light switch on the wall and a floor lamp next to the couch jumped to life. It was a good reading lamp, and he said so.

"I got you the Lord of the Rings trilogy," Jaden said. "I think you'll like it. It's a great story about running away. Really it's about how you can't run away. All you do is fulfill your destiny."

Josh plunked himself down on the couch, looked around, and saw a fat black spider resting on a web in the corner of the ceiling. "Some destiny."

"Well, it'll heat things up with your parents." Jaden ignored the spider and sat down next to him. She pushed her frizzy hair behind one ear, exposing her long neck and those thick, dark eyelashes.

"It's already pretty hot. They really went at it." He told her what happened.

She put a hand on his shoulder. "I'm sorry, Josh. It sounds terrible. Maybe you should go back. I'm not one hundred percent sure this is the right thing in the first place, especially because it was Benji's idea."

"It was a good idea on the bus." His voice came out angrier than he intended.

"On the bus they hadn't had this big blowout," she said. "I don't know if you can even bring them together now."

"Well, I'm not going back."

"You can't stay here forever," she said.

"You think I don't know that?" He glared at her and kicked the duffel bag on the floor.

"Then what?" She was not flustered.

"I don't know. Benji's place, then maybe Bricktown." Josh recalled the young men on the street corner. He knew most of them didn't have families, either. "I'll join a gang and live with the rest of them."

Jaden waved her hand. "That's the stupidest thing I've heard."

"Well! I know it's stupid, but I'm stupid right now, okay?"

Jaden got up and headed for the door. She stopped and turned around. "I think you should go home. I won't make you. I'll go along with whatever you want, Josh, but I think if you go back right now, this will all turn out better. There. I said it."

They stared at each other in silence, battling wills.

"Well?" Jaden finally asked.

Rain thrashed the tiny rectangular window in the corner of the room, and the house above them groaned beneath the wind.

Josh wanted to scream. He wanted to cry. He wanted to hug Jaden, but she was standing too far away.

He opened his mouth to tell her all those things.

"Good night" was all he said.

CHAPTER ELEVEN

JOSH AND JADEN DIDN'T talk when she brought him her Lord of the Rings paperbacks. She put the boxed set down on the end cushion and retreated up the steps. He took the first book, *The Fellowship of the Ring*, from the box and began to read about wizards and hobbits and elves, relieved to be lost in a scary wood, distracted from the ruin of his own life. At first the musty smell of the couch invaded his brain, but as the book and the night went on, his nose quit complaining. The boiler chugged away from behind the wall. The couch grew warm and cozy as the rain raged on against the window, and Josh caught himself drifting off. He reached up for the switch, put out the light, and fell into the black emptiness of sleep.

* * *

Somewhere in the night, an angry sound wrenched Josh awake.

He had no idea where he was or what was happening. In the total darkness nothing made sense. Then he remembered where he was—Jaden's basement. He remembered the warnings Benji gave on the bus about staying alone and break-ins. He saw furious, staggering shapes on the walls.

Josh bucked and fought to free himself from the fear.

He heard Jaden cry out.

The light went on, and footsteps thundered down the steps.

The face he saw terrified him.

CHAPTER TWELVE

"YOU THINK YOU CAN just *run away?"* Josh's father demanded.

"I . . ."

Josh's father raised a mighty paw to strike his face. Josh went limp. There was no use struggling against the power of a lion. When the blow came, all Josh felt was its breath. His father's hand slammed the cushion next to his head, sending a storm of dust swirling through the yellow cone of light from the reading lamp.

"You *what?* You *what,* Josh?" His father shook Josh's neck like it was a feather. "You like scaring your mother half to death? Scaring me?"

"No." Josh could barely speak.

Jaden stood by the door in her nightgown and robe, holding herself tight with both arms. She looked frightened or angry or maybe both.

"Ahhgg!" His father cast him loose. Seeing Josh's phone on the arm of the couch, he snatched it. "I'm taking this phone. You're not having a phone."

Josh sank into the couch. His father stamped around the small room with hands flying in wild circles above his head as he spoke. "You're impossible. Things are falling apart, and you're running away! Is that what you think life is about? Things get tough and you run!"

Josh might have been a marionette on strings, yanked suddenly upright, his jaw opening and closing without his control, words spilling from his mouth that couldn't have been his. "You're the one running!"

His father spun on him, cobra quick, and got in his face. "*I* am not *running*. I have a *job*."

"In Florida!" Josh shouted loud enough to make his father blink. "And Mom won't go!"

"That's her choice, not mine!" His father gripped his shoulders and shook him some more. "You're coming with me now. The decision has been made."

Josh felt so sick so suddenly, his stomach heaved. Jaden gasped.

"Come on." His father snapped his fingers at Josh. "Get up. Let's go. We'll get your things from home in the morning and go."

"Go?"

"They want me to start right away, and the sooner we're there, the sooner you'll be locked down." Josh's father stood to his full height so that the hair on his head brushed the ceiling.

"Mr. LeBlanc, can't Josh—" Jaden started.

Josh's dad spun around, and he pointed at Jaden with a trembling finger. "Nothing from you, young lady. You? I thought you had better sense than this. I can only imagine how disappointed your father will be."

That arrow hit home, and Jaden's face crumpled. She was starting to cry, but she swiped the tear away. Josh hadn't seen her so upset before, and it made him sicker still.

"Now," his father said to him, snapping his fingers again. He picked up the Speed Hitter he'd bought so Josh could practice his stroke.

Josh slung the duffel bag over his shoulder and marched past Jaden and up the stairs. His father's thumping feet followed, and he could feel his threatening presence right behind him. He wanted to apologize to Jaden. When he hesitated at the door, his father flung it open and shoved him out onto the porch. Jaden appeared in the light of the doorway.

"Josh!" She dashed out onto the porch. The robe clung to her body, her nightgown edge flapping in the cold wind. She held out the box of books. "Take these. Read them. You'll be okay. It'll be okay."

Josh took the books as his father tugged him down the steps so hard he nearly fell. The Camaro had one wheel over the curb and was planted in the grass.

The driver's door hung open. Headlights burned white through the streaks of rain. A cloud of exhaust huffed in the night. Josh opened his door, tossed the duffel bag in back, and climbed in, still clutching the books.

His father cursed the wet seat, slammed his door, and held his phone to his ear.

"Hello?" His voice was gruff. He started the engine. "Yeah. I got him. . . .

"Go ahead, Laura, blame me!" his dad yelled. "I really don't care at this point!" His father's voice continued to rise. "Yes, I'll keep him with me, and we'll be by in the morning for his things. . . . Good night to you too!"

His father slapped the phone down on the console between them and stepped on the gas. The rear of the car shrieked and wavered. They rocketed down the street. His father punched through a yellow light. They hit a bump, and Josh's head banged the ceiling.

"Ow!"

"Sorry." His father spoke low, and he did sound sorry. He slowed down and drove more normally. "What were you thinking?"

"How did you know I was there?"

"I didn't," he said. "I thought you were at Benji's."

Josh forgot himself and struck the dashboard. "He's unbelievable."

"What did you think? I wouldn't find you?" His father's voice exploded with anger again. "You scared your mother half to death."

"Oh, now you care about *her*?"

The car screeched to a stop, tires burning even on the wet road. Josh's ribs banged against his seat belt. His father had a hand on the back of Josh's neck and a look so wild in his eyes that Josh felt a moment of panic. Bright headlights suddenly lit up the car. They grew closer fast, and a truck's horn blared.

It was speeding right at them.

CHAPTER THIRTEEN

HIS FATHER WAS TOO mad to see, but he let go of Josh and smashed the gas pedal.

The car jerked forward. When the truck hit them they spun like a ride at the fair, jumped the curb, and nearly tipped over before rocking to a halt on the grass beneath a billboard.

"Are you okay?" His father's voice quavered, and he touched Josh's shoulder.

Josh pulled away, trembling, with the vise grip still burning in his brain. He nodded that he was okay, too mad and too shaken to speak.

"Okay," his father said, and got out of the car to look at the damage in the back.

The truck had pulled over, and the driver jumped down from his cab and jogged toward their car. Josh watched his father and the driver talking heatedly, ignoring the downpour. They exchanged cards, and Josh's father marched back and climbed in. Josh thought about asking if the accident was his fault too, but his neck reminded him to keep quiet.

They rode in silence out to his father's shabby, two-bedroom, first-floor apartment in the suburbs. When Josh got out, he eyed the crumpled rear quarter of the car and knew how badly that must burn his father. Josh thought he loved the car more than anything, even his family.

It had been a big deal—and a lot of money—early in the summer when his father had gotten a sponsorship contract from Nike to coach the Titans. Buying the car was the first thing his father had done to celebrate. By Josh's reckoning, the second was to get a girlfriend. His dad splurged on things his mother hadn't approved of. That was when they were still married. Now that they were divorced, she said his spending made her sick. Josh understood why. Since his father had left their home and gotten his own place, money had been in short supply.

Josh ground his teeth and followed his father through the parking lot and in the front doorway. The second bedroom had a single mattress on the floor and a sleeping bag. Josh tossed his duffel bag down and lay on the makeshift bed without taking off his sneakers. He doubted he would sleep.

After a few minutes he heard a knock at the door to their apartment. Josh hopped up and pressed his ear to the bedroom door. In the living room, his father and Diane Cross, the girlfriend, were talking. Josh didn't like Diane, but she wasn't the worst person he'd ever known, either. Her son, Marcus, had played with Josh on a Little League team earlier in the summer. Josh started out hating him, but eventually they'd become almost friends.

He never thought he'd feel sorry for Diane until he heard her voice.

"You can't just *leave*, Gary."

"I told you this might happen." His father's voice rumbled. "I told you it was coming together fast. It's an incredible opportunity. They're spending millions on the facilities, and I'm in on the ground floor."

"What about *me*?" she asked. "I can't just *leave*. My business is finally taking off, and Marcus is doing well in his school."

"I understand all that." His father's voice softened. "Not right now, but maybe you can work things out over the next few months or so. Sell your house. Come down there with me."

Josh wanted to puke. He couldn't imagine Diane and Marcus coming with them. Things were bad enough as it was. He opened the door a crack.

"I don't know, Gary," she said.

His father put his arm around Diane, stroking her

hair, saying, "I can't have you upset."

Josh brightened, thinking she'd convince his father to stay. Then she began to cry, and Josh worried himself sick all over again that his father might get her to come along with them. Where would Josh sit? In the back of that Camaro with Marcus? All the way to Florida? Josh was six feet tall. He didn't think he could fit—even alone—in that backseat.

He grabbed his hair and pulled.

His life was in ruins.

He heard Diane whimpering and his father's reassuring voice, but could no longer make out anything they were saying. After a while he lay back down, staring at the ceiling. On and on they talked while he waited, wondering what the outcome would be.

CHAPTER FOURTEEN

JOSH AWOKE WITH A start. Sun leaked through the gray army blanket covering the window. Outside, the sound of someone trying to start a dying engine set the tone for the day. He could see nothing ahead but exhausted failings. Only the urgent need to use the bathroom outdid his need to know what happened with Diane and his father. He looked around the bathroom as he went. A heap of towels lay on the floor. The sink and the tub were dirty. His mother would never allow such things.

He skipped washing his hands and made a beeline for the kitchen. His father already had a steaming mug of coffee in front of him along with his cell phone and a pad of paper. He jotted a note and looked up.

"So," Josh said, looking around. "Where's Diane?"

"Oh, you heard us?" His father raised his eyebrows.

"Well, she was crying."

His dad sighed. "Yes, and she's probably still at it. I broke it off."

"You're just leaving her?" Josh tried to wrap his head around it. He'd split up their family for her and now it was over? But Josh was glad it was over.

"I told you; this is the chance of a lifetime," his father said. "I really like Diane, but this is my dream, Josh. It'll help you with your dream too. Trust me. I know it seems hard right now."

With his father in a calm mood, Josh thought about asking for his phone back, but he decided not to push his luck.

"There's cereal and some milk in the fridge." His dad pointed to his notepad with his pen. "I'm tying up a few loose ends this morning. I thought we'd swing by the house a little before noon, get your things together, and get right on the road. We can be in North Carolina by midnight, stop for some sleep, and be at Crosby by tomorrow afternoon."

Josh froze. This was really happening, right now, not in some distant point in the future. Life as he knew it was about to end.

"What about your car?" Josh made the best play he could think of to stall their trip.

"The car runs. I'll fix it when I get down there." His father took a swig of coffee. "Don't look so surprised. Your little stunt last night sealed the deal. I was going to go down and get things set up by myself, but your mother's not going to go for that. She says she can't control you . . . not that I can, either, apparently."

His father went back to his phone and his notes. He dialed and began a conversation with the landlord about ending his lease early. Josh put some Raisin Bran in a bowl and splashed it with milk. When he returned the carton to the fridge, he noticed a hunk of cheese bearded with green and white mold. His stomach turned, but he put his bowl down at the table and sat poking at the raisins, taking a nibble now and then to justify him sitting there.

When his father got off the phone, Josh said, "If Mom lets me stay, can I?"

His father narrowed his eyes at Josh. "You mean stay, stay? Or just until I get set up?"

Josh poked at a raisin floating solo amid the milk and flakes. "I don't know."

"Well, this split-custody thing isn't going to work with me in Florida and your mom here. Your mom may cool off, but I think you need to go with me anyway, Josh." His dad began to make an intense little swirl of ink on the corner of his notepad. "You're not going to maximize your talent here with your mom, being coached by some nobody."

The tone of his father's voice didn't allow for Josh even to consider staying in Syracuse . . . but if he could prolong his stay, maybe he could get his mind ready for it, say good-bye to his friends, research the school he'd be going to and the baseball team he might play on down in Florida. "Just so I can say good-bye."

"Maybe for a little bit, but you'll have to be down there by the time school starts next week, and if you do stay and you pull a stunt like you did last night, I'll come up here and thrash you myself." His father's face grew so dark, the spoon slipped from Josh's fingers and clattered against the bowl.

"Yes, sir." He cast his eyes at the cereal.

"Well." His dad poured himself more coffee. "I'll ask your mother, but judging by how upset you made her, I wouldn't get my hopes up if I were you."

Josh let out a sigh of relief. His mother was soft. He could work on her; he knew he could. He got up and rinsed his bowl. He wanted to be a pro baseball player so much that it hurt. He wanted to do what his father hadn't quite been able to do. He had worked hard to get to this point, and he knew his dad was the best person to show him the path, but the thought of just going to Florida away from his best friends and his teammates scared him. When they played in Tampa at the Sunshine Tournament, they stayed in a motel near a swamp. The heat never let up, and the air conditioner—maxed out round the clock—mostly lost its battle to keep their motel room cool.

"Put that in the dishwasher." His dad was dialing his phone again. "I'll run it before we leave."

Josh did as he was told, then began a series of disgusting jobs meant to recover as much of his father's security deposit as possible. He told Josh he wanted the apartment cleaner than when he'd taken it over, and it sure looked as if there hadn't been much cleaning going on since then. So Josh got to work. He knew how to clean. His mother had taught him so he could help out after his father left home and she began working for a catering company.

As he scrubbed and vacuumed and wiped, he sensed that he was cleaning his way back into his father's good graces. That was his goal for two reasons. First, he wanted to work his way out of the trouble he'd gotten into by running away. Second, he wanted his father's full cooperation when Josh begged his mother to let him stay.

By eleven thirty the place was pretty clean. Josh helped his dad stuff the trunk of the Camaro with his things, surprised at how few possessions the man owned. His father cursed out loud when the damaged trunk wouldn't close, but he borrowed a bungee cord from the guy who did apartment maintenance and they were on their way.

Josh never loved his neighborhood as much as he did that day driving up to his house with the prospect of having to leave it.

Inside, his mother scowled, clicked her tongue, and

shook her head at Josh. That was it. She was so mad she couldn't speak. Josh put on the saddest, sorriest face he could come up with. "I'm sorry, Mom."

He nearly choked on his words. He could hear the TV, and when Laurel shut it off and tumbled into the kitchen to hug him, he nearly cried.

"Joshy! Joshy! Joshy!" She squealed the way three-year-olds do and kissed his face. "Don't run away, Joshy! Don't be bad!"

Josh shushed her and asked her if she wanted to play Candyland. She howled with delight.

"No chewing the cards," he said gently, looking up at his mom. "Mom, Dad says I can stay if it's okay with you. I won't do anything stupid. I'm not ready to go right now."

She bit her lip and looked at Josh's father before dashing out of the kitchen and up the stairs. Josh's dad frowned.

"Please, Dad."

"Play with your sister. I'll see what I can do." His father nearly had to duck to get through the doorway, and he thumped up the stairs.

Josh brought Laurel into the den and took Candyland off the shelf. Laurel chose the green piece. Josh took red and set things up. Before he could even take his first roll, Laurel had a card in her mouth.

Josh snatched it. "No, Laurel! How many times do I

have to tell you?" His voice rose. "Can't you just *listen*?"

Laurel's little face crumpled, and she began to bawl. Josh heard footsteps above, then on the stairs. He jumped up off the floor and hugged his little sister to get her to stop crying, but she only cried louder.

CHAPTER FIFTEEN

JOSH'S MOM GRABBED LAUREL from him, and her face went sour. "What did you do?"

Panic filled him. "Nothing! I told her not to chew the cards, *okay?*"

Laurel cried harder.

"Don't back talk me, mister!" Grim, his mother turned to his father. "You see? *This* is what I'm talking about, Gary. I can't control him."

Josh felt his insides melt. "Mom, please."

"Now it's please?" She clutched Laurel like a pillow and spoke harshly. "No, sir. You're going with your father. I don't need you bullying your little sister, running off in the middle of the night. I'm sorry, Josh. You need a father. Even yours."

"Get your things, Josh." His father was impatient.

"No." Josh shook his head, fighting back tears. "I don't want to just go. I can't just go. I have to . . ."

"Get your *things*, Josh!" His father slammed a palm against the wall. Knickknacks on the shelf danced and rattled. A porcelain mother duck with six chicks in tow tumbled to the floor along with a framed wedding picture of Josh's grandparents.

"*You!*" His mother scrambled for the pieces.

"Now!" His father yelled.

Josh took off up the stairs. He yanked another big duffel bag from his closet and emptied his drawers, cursing under his breath. He stuffed his best sneakers and the only pair of shoes he had into the pile of underwear, shorts, T-shirts, sweat pants, sweatshirts, and jeans. The bag was nearly full by the time he stopped to survey his bookcase. There were so many books, and he couldn't pick just one. He thought of the boxed set Jaden had given him, grateful for something to read. They had to have libraries in Florida, didn't they? He decided they did.

On top of his bookcase stood his trophies. There were many. They gleamed, golden and proud. He looked at the bag. He couldn't bring them all. Maybe just one? He selected the MVP from the national championship in Cooperstown, tucked it into the middle of his clothes for protection, and zipped the duffel bag shut. Throwing his comb and a few toiletries into his backpack, he slung it over his shoulder, then hoisted the duffel bag with both hands. He thumped his way out the bedroom door, turning around in the hall for one last look.

Heroes like Derek Jeter, Robinson Cano, and Jason Giambi graced the posters and team photos randomly covering the walls of his tiny room. The single bed in the corner was unmade, and Josh wondered if he'd ever bump his head on the low, sloping ceiling again. He tried to feed his anger, hoping it could overcome the hysterical desire to start crying, throw himself face-down on the bed in a tantrum, and refuse to go.

"Stupid bed," he said. "For a baby."

Then he turned his back on the best part of his childhood and marched down the stairs, right past his mother in the living room, and out the kitchen door-way. He didn't stop until everything was shoved into the backseat of the Camaro. He slipped into the front seat and slammed the passenger door. He sat with his arms folded across his chest, aware that his father was coming out of the house now.

His dad opened the driver's door and leaned in. "You better say good-bye."

"She wants me to leave?" The words even tasted bit-ter. "Fine, I'm leaving."

Josh's dad sighed and looked at the door leading into the kitchen. He stood there for several minutes, wait-ing, but Josh didn't move and his mother didn't appear. Somewhere inside, Josh could still hear his little sister howling. She got that way sometimes. She was sensitive.

Deep down, she probably knew Josh was leaving and, more important, her daddy was leaving too.

Josh nearly choked as his father started the engine. They backed out into the street and then took off. At the last instant Josh looked up at his house. There in the window stood his mother, Laurel clinging to her neck. Even through the window and from the street, Josh could see she was crying. And as his father stepped on the gas, his mother slowly raised her hand in what might have been a wave before the neighbors' bushes stole the sight of her from him.

CHAPTER SIXTEEN

IT DIDN'T SEEM REAL.

Every time Josh nodded off and woke with a jump, his head bumping the car window, he was sure it all must have been a bad dream. But as he sorted out his memories and emotions beneath the big green signs whooshing past, welcoming them to the states of Pennsylvania, Maryland, and Virginia, he knew it really had happened. His father really took a job in Florida. He really did ruin any chance of saying good-bye or preparing himself by running away, and his mother had shunned him in a way he never imagined possible. It all hurt so bad that he let himself drift back into sleep, over and over.

When they stopped at a Budget Host motel in North Carolina, Josh shuffled out of the car, bones aching from being cramped in such a small space, and collapsed into the bed his father pointed to after using the bathroom. They needed to be on the road by 5:00 a.m. He dropped off to sleep immediately.

The next morning Josh was still quiet. They had waffles and eggs at a Waffle House before getting back onto the highway with a bag of ham-and-egg sandwiches for lunch so they wouldn't have to stop.

After a few miles a question popped into Josh's mind without a warning, and without a thought he asked it. "Did you ever get used to leaving your teammates?"

"What do you mean?" his father asked.

"You know; you were at a lot of places. You must have had friends, right?"

"Some good ones, yeah." His father nodded with a smile.

"And then you left, right? Or they did."

"Sure, that's sports."

"Was there ever someone who was so awesome, you never found anyone like him?" Josh was thinking about Benji, and Jaden too, but he didn't want to say "him or her." He'd moved before. They moved a few times during his father's quest to become a major-league player. This wasn't Josh's first time by a long shot, but somehow it felt different. He'd never felt as close to someone as he did to Benji and, he had to admit, Jaden. How much of that was because she was a girl, and a pretty one at that, he couldn't say.

He looked over at his father, whose height and bulk filled most of the Camaro's space.

"Hmm," his father said. "I guess . . . no, not really. I made a lot of good friends, but there was always someone new."

Josh bit his lip, thinking of his mother and then Diane. He supposed there could be someone new like Diane for his father again, but for Josh it didn't seem like anyone could replace Benji, or especially Jaden. He didn't think there were too many people who were as crazy as Benji and at the same time . . . lovable? Josh supposed that was the word. Benji just got under your skin. And Jaden? He doubted there were many girls in the world who were as strong and smart as she was *and* who were also so . . . pretty. Yes, Jaden was about as pretty as a girl could get.

Josh sighed and put his head against the window.

"Don't tell me you're going to sleep again," his dad said without taking his eyes off the road.

"Tired, I guess." Josh reclined the seat as far as the stuff in the back would let him go. What he didn't tell his dad was that it was sadness really that had overcome him. A sadness about his friends that weighed him down, making his limbs and eyelids heavy.

Meanwhile, the vibration of the car and the steady thump of the road lulled him into a nap.

Sometime later, with the sun shining bright and directly down on him, he woke. Try as he might, he couldn't get back to sleep. He twisted and turned and kept his eyes shut for nearly half an hour before he sat up blinking.

"You got some rest." His father's voice rumbled deeply, like an extension of the car's engine, and he smirked at Josh. "Running away makes you tired, I guess."

"Where are we?"

"Florida-Georgia line."

"Like the band?"

"Like the band." His father reached for the dial and turned up the radio. "I didn't want to wake you."

The country band wasn't playing. It was some classic rock station, and the band was harsh and sour and singing a song with blaring guitars called "Highway to the Danger Zone." Josh looked sharply at his dad to see if he got the meaning, but his dad simply bobbed his head and sang along under his breath as they buzzed beneath a sign welcoming them to the Sunshine State. Josh blinked up at the glaring yellow orb.

Florida.

No doubt about the sunshine.

"Hey." His father glanced at his watch and reached for the radio again. "One o'clock. Yankees are playing the Dodgers today. You gotta love this satellite radio, huh? I think they have a channel for everything."

The game came on, and they listened together, both of them intent on the action and the suspense. Josh pulled out the sandwiches, and they ate as they listened. The announcer said the day was overcast in New York, but it seemed impossible that the sun Josh and his dad drove beneath could be hidden by anything, so intense were its rays. Josh directed the AC vent toward his face. In the bottom of the second inning, the Dodgers left fielder Max Zumwalt stepped up to the plate. He was a player Josh hadn't heard of, and when he turned his attention to his dad to ask about him, he was surprised by the open-mouthed look of shock on his father's face.

"What is it?" Josh asked, scanning the road ahead of them. "Did something happen?"

CHAPTER SEVENTEEN

JOSH'S DAD HUFFED AND clucked his tongue, shaking his head now in disbelief as he reached to turn up the radio. "Max Zumwalt. I can't even believe it."

"Who is it, Dad? You know him?"

"Shh." His father held up a hand, and they listened as Zumwalt swung and missed.

Puzzled and curious, Josh held his questions until Zumwalt ripped a single on the third pitch and his father dropped his hand, glancing at Josh with a grin that appeared to be crooked with pain.

"Who is he?" Josh asked.

"That could have been me." His dad glanced at Josh again, serious now. "I swear, that could have been me, Josh. That's how close things are in life, especially in sports."

"What do you mean?" Josh asked.

"I mean, he and I played together on a Double-A team in Manchester." His father shook his head, still in disbelief. "They moved him down because his batting average was like .147. Meanwhile, I got bumped *up* to Triple-A and played for the Chiefs."

"I don't get it," Josh said.

"He went *down* and ended up playing for Dino Wellington. You know the name?"

It rang a bell, but Josh shook his head.

"Back then Wellington was a kid fresh out of college with a good eye. He coached in the minors awhile, and *now* he's the Dodgers hitting coach." Josh's father struck the wheel with one hand and glanced over at him. "See what I mean? About luck?"

"I still don't get it." Josh furrowed his brow.

"Zumwalt went *down*. I went *up*." His father spit out the words. "But *up* wasn't the right place to be. I remember hearing Zumwalt got his bat straightened around by Wellington. Maybe Wellington gave him some mojo? Whatever it was, now Zumwalt's in Yankee Stadium playing for the Dodgers, and I'm driving a wrecked Camaro down I-95."

Josh digested that as they drove along, still listening to the game. He couldn't help rooting against Zumwalt and the Dodgers even more than normal because the whole thing didn't seem fair. If his father was better, it should be him playing today, not Zumwalt. Josh's dad had told him over and over about the luck factor when it came to sports, but part of him hadn't really believed it. Now he did, and the injustice of it added a slightly bitter taste to what was otherwise a super afternoon: riding along listening to a ball game with his dad.

The game ended with the Dodgers winning 3–2 before his father turned the radio down and nodded toward the side of the road. "Beautiful, isn't it?"

Josh looked out the window at the endless line of trees, some slung with creepy moss that reminded him of a monster movie. "It's green."

"Yup." His dad nodded with excitement. "Green and lush and warm. No snow. No shoveling. No winter boots or coats or hats. I love it."

Josh took a deep breath and let it out, his second thoughts about coming continued to grow. He did get excited when he saw a sign for Disney World, though, and he pointed it out to his dad. "Can we go?"

"After we get settled in. Why not?"

"Awesome."

When they finally pulled through the gates of Crosby College late that afternoon, Josh couldn't help being impressed. The place had the feel of a park, with trees and lush green grass that defied the heat. Brick buildings boasted thick white columns and windows and felt like they'd been around for a hundred years.

"What's that called?" Josh pointed to the top of one

building and the fancy monument with a clock and a dome-shaped roof with a gold weathervane.

"A cupola."

"Coop-o-la?"

"Yup."

"Fancy." Josh put his hand on the window. "Where do we stay?"

"In one of the dorms for now," his father said. "Just until my place is ready. Jeff's got an apartment all lined up."

Josh gave his father a puzzled look.

"Mr. Enslinger, Jeff," his father said. "I already texted him last night when you were sleeping. He's working on getting you into the Marberry School and on the Cougars travel team too. I wanted him to find something close, but I also want to make sure you're going to a good school. My goal is to be in the apartment this weekend so we're settled before school starts Monday. Most of the college students won't be here until then, either, so it'll be pretty quiet. I can get my office set up, and we should be able to do some work in the weight room and out on the field, a little one-on-one with the head coach. It's been a while, right?"

Josh and his dad used to do one-on-one work regularly until his father's career as a minor-league player ended and he began his coaching career. Not that his dad didn't work with him, they'd worked together plenty. It was just that the attention wasn't on an individual basis like before. His dad had been coaching him along with all the other players on the Titans team.

They drove past the impressive buildings that lined the main street of the campus, then circled the biggest building of all before they came to a modern, three-story building surrounded by sports fields.

"My office is in there." Josh's dad nodded his head toward the big building. "Weight room too. Locker rooms."

They passed through a line of trees before Josh saw all the action on the baseball field. A big construction crew was working, some on the field, others on the enormous grandstand. Huge yellow machines coughing dust crawled across the dirt, grumbling and snorting black smoke.

"It's a little messy now, but wait until you see the plans." His father surveyed the action, and his eyes brimmed with excitement. "They're gonna upgrade everything over the next couple years. This is just the beginning. I'll get better players, and we'll start to win. I'll get even better players after that, and Crosby College will become a Division One powerhouse. It'll be a training ground for the majors."

Josh's dad waved his hand like a magic wand intended to make the whole dream appear.

The Camaro wound its way through twists and turns

until they came upon a huge building that made Josh blink in disbelief.

His father laughed with appreciation and uttered just two words.

"Welcome home."

CHAPTER EIGHTEEN

JOSH'S FATHER CALLED Jeff Enslinger to tell him they'd arrived. The brick building looked even more impressive when they walked over to find the athletic director waiting for them at the door with open arms and a smile. He hugged Josh's dad. "This is a great day for Crosby College."

"I don't know about that."

Josh couldn't remember seeing his father blush, and as unhappy as he was about the turmoil in his life and leaving everything behind, he was proud of his dad.

They climbed the stone steps and passed through the white double doors. The AD led them down a wood-paneled hallway and swung open the door to room 104. "Not much, but it'll keep you dry until your new place is ready this weekend."

Josh's father was right; he was in heaven.

"It's an RA's room, so it's got its own bathroom." The AD pointed to a doorway inside the room. "A little tight because I had them put in an extra bed, but you guys will be like two buddies living together. Ha. I'll let you get settled and meet you in the dining hall. We can have an early dinner."

Josh's father had carried a duffel bag with him, and after shaking the AD's hand, he set it on one of the two single beds that rested against opposite walls.

Josh peeked into the bathroom, cramped but neat and clean with a sparkling mirror, white fixtures, and a black-and-white checkered tile floor. "Nice."

"See?" His father watched the AD disappear down the hallway. "This is my big chance."

Josh tugged open the blinds and admired the big oak tree and the closely trimmed grass outside their window.

"Just two buddies living together." His dad laughed. "Sounds funnier when he says it with that Southern accent."

"Two buddies *training* together too." Josh was excited about working out on a daily basis with his dad, getting bigger, faster, stronger, and more skilled.

"I hope you can handle working like a Division One player." His father bumped into him with a shoulder, and Josh bumped him back.

"I hope I don't wear you out." Josh grinned, his

sadness about leaving Syracuse almost entirely gone.

They unpacked and headed for the dining hall. It was nearly empty, but there were enough college students dressed in shorts, T-shirts, and sandals to make Josh feel out of place. The students offered up plenty of smiles, but Josh also caught them staring, wondering who was with the AD.

"How about this?" His dad held up a burrito before taking a big bite and talking through his food. "Not bad, right?"

"Good," Josh said.

His father's phone rang, and he fished it from his pocket, looked at the number, and hit Ignore. Josh wondered who it was but said nothing. His father smiled at the AD.

"The head of dining services came from Florida State." The AD bit into a tuna sandwich, crunching through a thick slab of white onion. "We're beating them in the dining hall, and soon we'll be beating them on the baseball diamond."

"We're a long way from taking on Florida State." Josh's dad took a drink of his Dr Pepper. "I figured the construction would be further along. There's a lot of competition for the top recruits. Telling them we're going to have big-time facilities is different than them *seeing* big-time facilities, especially when you're competing for the best kids."

"What? Against a guy like you, Gary?" The AD

grinned through his food. "I know you can sell these kids. When you walk into some kid's living room and the dad is full of questions and the mom is fluttering her eyes at you, you're gonna *sell* them. I know it. You've got that thing . . . that X factor."

Josh looked at his dad. He'd never thought about it that way, but it was true. His dad was intimidating; but at the same time everyone's mom seemed to like being around him, and he'd noticed how they let their eyes linger on his dad whether he was talking about a kid's need to get more sleep or what the bus schedule for an away trip was going to be. He'd seen his dad sell people.

"How much recruiting do you have to do?" Josh asked his dad.

His father shrugged and looked at the AD. "A couple days a week on the road, I guess."

The AD stopped just before he took another big bite of his tuna sandwich, and his bright smile faded a little. "Well . . . uh, no. You'll be on the road six or seven days a week, Gary."

Josh looked at his dad, who scratched the stubble on his chin. "But a lot of the kids I'll be recruiting are right around here."

"Oh, for sure." The AD nodded. "Miami, Fort Lauderdale, Tampa, there's even a lot of good talent right here around Orlando, but you'll be spending a lot of time in Texas."

"Texas?" Josh said.

"Tons of talent in Texas, and on your way, there's no sense not stopping in Mississippi and Louisiana too." The AD took a big bite, crunching more of the thick onion and chewing happily. "I'm so glad you're on board."

Josh's dad only smiled and ate.

After that Josh zoned out while the two of them talked about places to live and the strengths and weaknesses of the existing Crosby College baseball team. But Josh's mind was on Texas and how much traveling his dad would be doing.

Josh put down his second taco only half eaten. The "two buddies" living together in a college dorm, working out and training for baseball, suddenly vanished like smoke. He'd probably end up living mostly on his own, but would that even be possible? Someone had to look after him, hadn't they? Right now he had no friends and no teammates in sight. Of course he'd be in school soon and on a team, but there were no guarantees he'd even like the new kids. He hadn't been thinking about that part of things, and now there wasn't a thing he could do about it.

He realized he was breathing fast. He tried to take a drink of milk but choked on it. His father distractedly thumped his back while he kept talking. Josh could only think of one thing. Jaden.

He needed to talk to Jaden. She'd know. She was the smartest person he'd ever met, and not just with books but with people. He needed to call her, but he still had no phone. He poked his father without thinking whether the timing was right or not, only knowing that Jaden was the only person who might be able to think of a solution.

"What, Josh?" His father's voice was restrained.

"Can I . . . ?"

"Can you what, Josh? We're talking."

"Can I have my phone? I need to make a call."

CHAPTER NINETEEN

HIS DAD FROWNED, BUT reached into his pocket and handed Josh his phone. "Take it out there."

"Thanks." Josh left the two men to talk and let himself out through the glass doors onto a terrace overlooking a square of grass crisscrossed by brick sidewalks and spotted with palm trees. He sat on a bench but bounced up because the sun had turned it into a frying pan. He found a seat in the shade and sat down, dialing Jaden.

She answered, out of breath. "Josh? Are you okay? Where are you?"

"Did you get in trouble?" Josh asked.

"Your dad never said anything. My dad has no idea, and I'm not going to tell him. I figured you got your phone taken away."

"I still can't believe Benji told on us." Josh could just make out the shape of his dad talking to the AD through the reflection on the dining-hall window.

"Well, don't go too hard on him," Jaden said. "He told me his lips were sealed until his mom threatened to call his dad over that minute. It was like midnight, and the last time his dad got called over at midnight, he made Benji unload a pickup truck full of bricks and stack them in the driveway."

"He couldn't hold out for that?" Josh asked.

"His dad made him load it and unload it five times," she said. "He said his arms hurt for three weeks, and he was sure a fellow heavy hitter would forgive and forget."

Josh laughed. He rested his forehead in his free hand and bent into the phone. "So, listen, I got a problem."

He told her what had happened and how it looked like he was going to be stuck down in Florida, spending most of his time completely alone. "I mean, six or seven days a week."

She was quiet for a moment before speaking. "Well, you'll be in school soon, right? They start early down there."

"Yeah, it starts, like, next week," Josh said.

"And you're going to be on a travel team, right?"

"Supposedly."

"So you're going to be busy, Josh," she said. "Trust me, I don't want you living down there. I can't stand not having you around. I can't believe it actually happened, and just like that."

Josh heard her snap her fingers.

"So, nothing. You don't have any ideas at all?" The heat pressed in on him.

"I'm sorry, Josh. Let me think, okay?"

"Sure."

"Hey, don't sound so glum. Look at the bright side."

"What bright side?" he asked.

"Well, you're with your dad," she said. "You're gonna be playing baseball; and if things go well for your dad, with the contacts he'll make, it'll put you that much closer to the majors. I mean, coaching a successful travel team is great, but a Division One coach? It can only help."

"I guess."

"Hey." Jaden sounded upbeat. "It might be great. Maybe the place you're getting has a pool. Lots of places have pools down there. We had one in Texas."

Josh remembered that Jaden had lived in Dallas, where her father had been studying to be a doctor. They'd moved to Syracuse after her mom died. Josh suddenly pictured Jaden on the bus with the worry beads. Was it only two days ago?

His father's call broke into his troubled thoughts.

"Here comes my dad, Jaden. I've got to go, but please think anyway."

"I will."

"And . . . Jaden?"

"Yeah."

"I miss you guys. I miss . . . *you.*"

The phone went silent.

CHAPTER TWENTY

FINALLY, JADEN SPOKE, AND Josh wished badly she wasn't a thousand miles away.

"Yeah," she said. "Me too."

Josh said good-bye and hung up just as his dad and the AD arrived. His father clapped his hands together and rubbed them like it wasn't broiling hot. "Okay, my friend. Let's look around the town. We can see where the apartment I got for us is before it gets too dark."

"Does it have a pool?" Josh didn't want to get his hopes up.

His dad looked at the AD.

"Sure," Mr. Enslinger said. "This is a really nice place, and they've got a pretty big pool. I think it even has one of those waterfalls and a slide."

"That's kind of awesome," Josh said.

They said good-bye to the AD, then returned to their dorm for the car.

Josh hesitated with his hand on the door handle. "Can I get the Speed Hitter? Maybe we can get some work in. Maybe the apartment complex has a grass area or something."

His father grinned. "Absolutely. You know what? Get your suit and a towel too. Maybe you can test out that slide at the pool."

"I can?"

"Why not?" his dad said.

"Well, we don't live there yet."

"I'll handle it if anyone asks." His father stood a little straighter, and Josh couldn't imagine that anyone would bother such a mountain of a man.

Josh ran into the dorm for his gear and a bathing suit, threw it all in the back, and climbed in. When his dad's phone rang, he looked at the number and hit Ignore again. It wasn't Josh's business who kept calling, but he had to wonder. He waited for his dad to say something, but his father cleared his throat and turned on the radio.

The complex wasn't too far away, and his dad explained that his school would be no more than a mile and he could walk. Josh didn't ask any more about that because he was trying not to think about the possibility that his dad wouldn't be around much. He'd try to take it a day at a time for now.

They drove past some housing complexes and a strip of stores and gas stations around a shopping center that also looked new before turning into the River Ranch Apartments. Josh wondered where the river was but kept quiet about that too. The place was nice: three-story clapboard buildings with white railings, gables, and steep roofs. There were beds of flowers and fresh green shrubs that defied the heat.

They got out of the car, and his dad said to bring his bathing suit. Crickets sang, and Josh was struck by the lack of people as they rounded one building into a courtyard area where the pool lay. "I wanted to show you the inside of the apartment, but it's still occupied. If this pool area is any indication, it's gotta be nice."

Josh looked around. A small waterfall hissed, and a modest mountain of concrete held a curving slide. No one else was around. Josh quickly changed in the men's room, then walked over to the pool slide while his father reclined in a chair beneath the roof of an eating area.

Josh hesitated at the top, but his father called out, "Go ahead!"

Josh went down, slipping and sliding and making a huge splash. He laughed as he surfaced in a flurry of bubbles.

"Fun?" his dad called.

"You bet!" Josh hurried out and up and slid back down, laughing as he did. The slide was a great novelty, and the water was cool enough to provide some relief from the evening heat. Some lights came on after a while, and Josh's dad said they'd better get going because one mosquito had bitten him already. Josh changed back into his clothes, and they were on their way to the dorm when he remembered the baseball gear.

"We didn't practice," Josh said.

"Well, you had fun, and you got to enjoy where we'll live. There's plenty of time for baseball." His dad pulled through the gates of Crosby College, and his phone buzzed another time before he silenced it. "Tomorrow we can see your new school in the morning, then work out, and then later we can meet your new team."

"My team?" Josh felt a thrill go through him. Florida was a baseball state, and even though they'd had plenty of success with the Titans, baseball was year-round in the Southern states.

"I told you you'd be playing for a travel team down here," his dad said.

"I know, but I didn't know it was settled," Josh said.

"The Crosby Cougars. Mr. Enslinger told me about them when you made your phone call. It's coached by a friend of his, Caden T. Helle. He used to play at TCU. The Cougars have done pretty well, but they'd love to have a second baseman who can hit like you."

From nowhere, lightning cracked and a white flash lit up the world. Rain began to pour down, and they had to scramble from the car to the dorm, laughing together. They got ready for bed before watching a movie on his dad's laptop. It was after midnight when Josh crawled into his own bed. His father shut off the lights, and the darkness was complete. Josh lay there, thinking how impossible it was to know how he felt. Images of Jaden, Benji, his father, Diane, his mom, the Crosby AD, and his sister, Laurel, swirled in his mind.

His father cleared his throat, and Josh's mind stopped spinning. "Tomorrow you'll meet the Cougars."

Josh felt suddenly proud and glad. The good thing about baseball was that wherever you were, the diamond was the same. The players might change, but the game was the game, pure and simple.

"Dad, could we end up playing the Titans?" He wasn't sure what made him think about it, but Josh thought it would be hard to play against his old team.

"The Titans?" His father cleared his throat. "No, I'm pretty sure the Cougars are in another fall ball league. It's NYBA or something, National Youth Baseball. Titans are in YBEL."

"Oh." Josh felt the pinch of disappointment, suddenly remembering the contest Benji had told him about. Since the Cougars weren't a YBEL team, he wouldn't have a chance at the Home Run Derby, which sounded pretty fun. The chance to win a better home for his mom wouldn't be a bad thing.

They lay quiet for a while before his dad spoke again.

"I don't want you to ever do it again, but honestly? I'm glad you ran away." His dad's words hung there in the black silence.

Josh swallowed. "You are?"

CHAPTER TWENTY-ONE

JOSH'S FATHER CHUCKLED. "WELL, yeah. I wanted you down here with me, Josh. I didn't want to do this alone. You and me? We're a team, right?"

Even though it ached a bit for his mom and little sister, Josh felt his heart swell with pride. No matter how his dad disappointed him, he was still his dad, a giant of a man who impressed people. Hadn't he been a first-round draft pick by the Mets? Didn't he lead his son's travel team to an impressive national championship and then get hired by a program heading for Division One?

"Yeah," Josh said, even with his words to Jaden about wanting to go home ringing in his ears. "We are a team, Dad. Always."

* * *

The next morning they went to the Marberry School. Josh and his dad met the principal and Josh's guidance counselor, both upbeat and friendly women. Josh got a quick tour—typical classrooms, cafeteria, and gym— and they registered him for classes. Josh looked at his schedule. It was the same as he'd had at Grant Middle in Syracuse; but he realized that this school was private, and he wondered about the money, even though he said nothing.

After that his dad took him to the ball diamond where the Cougars practiced, and they worked out for a while on the field. The storm from the night before seemed to have broken the intense heat and humidity, for a few hours anyway. Sunshine spilled down on them, and the breeze had just a touch of cooling power so that Josh had to work for his sweat. They got some lunch before his dad took him to a local batting cage that was sort of shabby. The pitching machine only worked well about half the time, and Josh had to duck a few errant pitches; it was like playing a game of dodgeball. They got some laughs out of the machine though, and Josh felt like his stroke had a nice rhythm.

On the way back to Crosby College, his dad drove by the River Ranch Apartments. The place looked even nicer than Josh remembered it. Josh's father's phone buzzed, and as he'd done all morning, he checked the number, hit Ignore, and stuffed the phone back into his pocket.

"The lap of luxury, right?" His father pointed at River Ranch and grinned.

Josh thought about the apartment and now the private school. "But we can afford it and the private school? It seems like a lot."

His father lost his grin for a split second, then forced it back into place and nodded his head. "Yup. I can make it happen."

Something about the way his father answered made Josh look back at the apartment complex and wonder if they really could afford it. He remembered the papers his mother had handed his father, the ones from the bank.

Josh had a sinking feeling that—nice as these apartments and the private school were—the two of them together were going to create problems he couldn't even imagine.

CHAPTER TWENTY-TWO

THE TRAVEL TEAM THE AD picked for Josh—the Crosby Cougars—practiced at the field Josh already had a flavor for. The day's heat had built on itself, and while the sun had disappeared behind a city of clouds, the air seemed to stick to Josh's skin. He marched up to Coach Helle with his dad that morning, both eyeing the players out on the field. There was no fooling around. Each group was involved in some kind of warm-up drill, either fielding grounders or working a long toss to loosen their arms.

"Caden? I'm Gary LeBlanc. Jeff Enslinger sent us."

Coach Helle was a bear of a man. He looked up from his clipboard, tucking his pen behind one small ear and welcoming them in a low, rumbling Southern voice, with handshakes and a smile.

He wore a cap, but Josh could see that he'd shaved his head, and his small, dark eyes in his big, meaty face looked Josh up and down. "Jeff said you had a big boy. I guess he wasn't kidding. He'll fit right in with this group. We draw from a fifty-mile radius, and I like my players big. Everyone but Declan Casper."

Coach Helle pointed to one boy who looked two years younger than the rest.

"Clocked his fastball at seventy-seven the other day. Thirteen years old. You want to sign him up now, Coach?" Coach Helle laughed.

"I might," Josh's dad said. "Can he mix it up at all?"

"He's got a nice curveball. Not much action on his slider, but we're working on it. Josh, you can get right into the mix. Casper! Long toss with our new guy!"

Declan Casper peeled off from his group of three and waved Josh over. Josh looked at his dad.

"Get to it," his dad said. "I'm gonna talk to Coach Helle, then head over to my office to make some calls and I'll be back."

Josh said very little to his new teammates, and they seldom spoke among themselves. That was fine with Josh. He fit right in and didn't hesitate to jump into drills. In the field, the other kids were every bit as skilled as Josh. They had quick reflexes, sure gloves, and strong arms.

When it came to batting, though, Josh stood out. At the end of practice, they each got ten pitches against a live defense. Coach Jones, the assistant coach, had only just graduated from a big baseball factory, the University of Central Florida. He threw the pitches right down the pipe.

When Josh stepped up to the plate for his turn, Coach Helle encouraged him.

"Okay, Josh. Let's see that bat I heard so much about."

Josh's new teammates were crouching and ready for a hit. Josh drilled the first pitch into the hole between first and second and took first base before jogging back for the next pitch. The second one was low and outside, and he missed, swinging for the fences. Josh felt hot shame, even though he shouldn't have. Every batter before him had at least several strikes.

The next one, Josh swung just as big. This time he connected, crushing the ball over the center-field fence.

"No sense running the bases." Coach Helle marked something on his clipboard. "Nice knock."

After they all brought it in for a team chant, Declan appeared beside Josh as he stuffed a bat inside his equipment bag.

"Hey, that was pretty good."

"Thanks." Josh looked up. Declan might be a friend, but before Josh got to do more than give him a cautious smile, Coach Helle barked his name.

"Josh, got a minute?" Coach Helle put a hand on

the frame of the dugout and leaned toward him before motioning to the bench.

"Sure." Josh took a seat and watched the remaining handful of players in the dugout scatter like mice.

Coach Helle sat down beside him and patted Josh's shoulder. "You're good with a bat, and I like your defense too."

Coach Helle continued, "I know you're used to having your dad be your coach, and I'm betting he didn't allow you to second-guess him. Am I right?"

Josh didn't have to hesitate on that one. "Right."

"Good." Coach Helle stood up. "I'm the same way, and it's kinda like that Las Vegas ad you see on TV. What happens in Vegas stays in Vegas, and what happens in Cougarland stays in Cougarland. No second-guessing. Got it?"

It wasn't a question. Josh thought about not talking over plays with his dad. His friends were a thousand miles away. His mom was a thousand miles away. If he couldn't talk to his dad, he had no one. He didn't want to just agree to something he had no intention of doing, but Coach Helle was staring and waiting, and Josh felt like whatever he said, it was going to have a big impact on him, and not just for this moment.

CHAPTER TWENTY-THREE

"MY DAD AND I are pretty close," Josh said.

He watched Coach Helle's unblinking eyes as they drilled down on him. Coach Helle spoke softly. "And that's a good thing. I'm just saying that I need to coach my way and you need to play my way, and I don't want to get into it with your dad. Now, he and I spoke, and he's on board, but I need you to be on board too."

"Oh, well, if you talked to my dad and he's good, I'm good." Josh felt he had no choice.

"Super." Coach Helle pointed at him. "You know, you're as good as they said. I know you just got here, but what do you think about playing with us in this tournament we've got Sunday? It's an overnight, but Tallahassee's not far. I'd like to get you right into the lineup."

Josh had mixed feelings. He wanted to dive right in, but they were supposed to move into their new apartment over the weekend. School began on Monday, and his father was already talking about a recruiting trip in the middle of the week. It was all happening so fast.

"I don't want to pressure you." Coach Helle held up his hands. "Just think about it. If you want to come, you can let me know tomorrow."

"Thanks, Coach." Josh followed him out of the dugout and saw his dad waiting in the parking lot.

Coach Helle waved to Josh's dad but got into his own green pickup without stopping to talk.

"So? How'd it go?" his dad asked.

"Really well." Josh told him about his hitting and didn't mention anything Coach Helle had said to him. He did tell his dad about the weekend tournament in Tallahassee, though.

"Hey, that's great."

"But we're moving into the new place, right?"

His dad steered out of the parking lot and onto the road. "Yeah, but that's no big deal. The rental company will deliver the furniture, and your stuff and mine together won't take any time to unload. No, you get things going with your team. That's great, right? I mean, a team is like a bunch of instant friends."

"Uh, yeah. That's right." Josh nodded to add support to his words even though only Declan had tried to be friends.

Josh didn't hear his father's phone ring, but because it was dark outside, when it lit up from its place on the charger cord, Josh saw it. His father snatched the phone and hit Ignore with a grunt of displeasure.

"Who is that?" Josh figured the noise his father made opened the door for a question.

"Nah. No one." His father waved his hand. "I must have given my number out to a marketing company or something. I'm always getting sales calls on this thing."

"Oh," Josh said. "Yeah, that's gotta be annoying."

As he spoke, another call came in, and his father hit Ignore and then powered the phone right down. "Ridiculous."

His father turned the music up, and they returned to their dorm room. Josh's dad was in the shower when his own phone vibrated. It was Jaden, texting to see if he could talk. Josh dialed her number.

"Hi, Josh."

"Hi," he said.

Jaden paused as if she was waiting for him to say something more than hello back to her. "Josh, is everything okay?"

The tone of her voice sent his heart thumping. "Yeah, I think so. Why?"

CHAPTER TWENTY-FOUR

"YOUR MOM DIDN'T SAY anything to you?" Jaden asked.

Josh huffed. "Jaden, I have no idea what you're even talking about! I haven't talked to my mom yet. My dad and I have been really busy."

"With your house." Her voice was as sad as it was sorry.

"What about my house?" The shower water went off in the bathroom, and Josh tried to keep his voice down.

"Oh, I'm sorry. I'm sorry. Benji told me not to call. Who listens to Benji, though, right?" Jaden said.

"Jaden! *What* are you talking about?"

"There's a For Sale sign in your front yard. I thought you knew. I'm so stupid. I was worried, but then I thought maybe your mom is coming down there. Josh, I was thinking that somehow you might come back. I know your mom was mad at you but . . ."

"Wait. What For Sale sign?" Josh was sick. "What are you talking about? Not for my house. Not my mom's house. It must be the neighbor."

"I don't know," she said, "maybe. They hung it right on your fence, though, but maybe. It said they're holding an auction. In two weeks."

Josh's father came out of the bathroom with a towel around his waist.

"I gotta go. I'll call you later." Without waiting for a reply, Josh hung up the phone. "Dad, are we selling our house? I mean, is Mom? The house in Syracuse?"

Josh's father didn't have to say a word. By the sorry, angry, sad look on his face, Josh knew it was true.

CHAPTER TWENTY-FIVE

JOSH'S FATHER SAT DOWN on the edge of his bed. He looked at his hands to avoid looking at Josh. "It's hard to explain everything. I've got a lot of pressure on me, right? I mean, this is a big move."

"What's that got to do with our house?" Josh couldn't believe what he was hearing, this mealymouthed nonsense about the pressure his dad was under.

"Your mother doesn't need a house that big, Josh." His dad scratched his shoulder. "She wasn't listening to anything I said, so I just stopped fighting with her about it, but I wasn't going to keep paying for it."

"What? You just stopped paying for our house? We live there!"

His dad looked around. "No, *we* don't live there. *We* live here, and we're going to move into one of those nice apartments with the water slide. I need a security deposit and the first month's rent. I've gotta get furniture, and it costs money up front to send you to private school and have you on a new travel team."

"Oh, yeah? And where is Mom going to go? And Laurel?" Josh tried not to scream, but he felt panic tightening like a thick rope around his neck.

"They can get an apartment like us, Josh." His father sounded calm and reasonable, almost comforting. "There's nothing wrong with living in an apartment. You don't have to worry about repairs. I lived in an apartment until I was fourteen. Plenty of people do."

Josh tried to catch his breath. "Dad, it's Mom and Laurel. They can't just live anywhere."

"Josh, I tried to get her to come down here. You heard me."

"She's got her job, and she *had* a house," Josh said.

"Maybe now, without the house, she'll think about coming down."

"Is that why you did it?" Josh couldn't believe it.

"No." His father shook his head violently. "I'd like her to move down so you and Laurel and she could spend time together, but she's not an easy woman, Josh."

"She's not easy? This is *Mom's* fault? She wasn't the one who got a girlfriend, Dad. That was you."

"Hey, mister. Watch your tone of voice with me." His father's face clouded over fast. His voice turned deep with the threat of a storm. "Where are you going?"

Josh was on his feet, phone in his hand. "I have to get out for a minute. I have to think."

"Fine," his father said. "You go think. That's how your mother handles things. I'm a doer, Josh. That was always part of the problem with me and your mother."

"Maybe that's part of my problem too, Dad. I'm not a doer, right? Maybe I'm like her. I guess I am." Josh flung the door open and tried not to slam it behind him, because he knew that would risk his father coming down on him like a brick building. He marched up the hallway, past a room with an open door where three college students sat on a bed playing cards with country-western music twanging in the background. Josh couldn't wait to be in college—or in the minors, taken in the MLB draft after high school. Anywhere, just to be on his own and away from his parents.

Outside he found a bench beneath a big oak tree sunken in shadows cast by the light from the lampposts, which stood like sentries along the walking paths. He slumped down and took out his phone. Emotions swirled in his brain. Part of him was furious with his mom for sending him away. Another felt horrible, like he was personally responsible for her losing her house as well as her family. Wasn't baseball something they'd fought about too?

His father was intent on Josh becoming a major leaguer, something he hadn't quite been able to do but something he felt Josh was destined for. His mother,

on the other hand, nagged constantly about the impor-
tance of school. Once she even went so far as to tell
Josh that she didn't want him to end up like his father.
As if that was something so bad? The idea burned Josh
from the inside out.

Still, almost as if his fingers could think for themselves, he dialed his mom's cell number.

She answered right away. "Josh?"

"Mom?" he said. "What's happening? Dad's making
you sell the house? He can't do that, can he? Can we
stop him?"

The line went silent for a moment. He heard his mom
take a deep breath and let it out slowly. "It's the bank
that's making me sell it, Josh. He stopped making the
payments. . . ." Her voice sharpened. "There is a way to
make him, though. Oh, I don't know, Josh. I don't want
to put you in the middle of it."

"I *am* in the middle of it, Mom. How? How can we
stop it?"

"Well, I'll tell you, Josh, but you may not like what
you have to do."

CHAPTER TWENTY-SIX

JOSH STOOD UP AND put his hand on the tree's rough bark, steadying himself against the immovable mass of the old tree.

His mother's voice was strained. "It's long and it's complicated, but the agreement your father and I have with custody of you kids says that he has to pay a certain amount of child support for you and a certain amount for Laurel. Do you understand?"

"No," Josh said. "What are you talking about?"

"If you live with me, your father—by law—has to pay me more money," she said.

"Enough to keep the house?" Josh asked.

"Enough to have a chance of keeping it. Without you and the support money, there's just no way. I already spoke to the bank. They're not going to wait. Your father has been making promises to the bank and breaking them for a while. The extra money we had from his Nike contract he already spent on that car and other stupid things. I asked Gran to help. She said she will, but only if I get you back and force your father to pay the full support."

"Force him?" Josh gripped the hair on top of his head. "What do you mean?"

"The court won't let him get behind on child support. They'll issue a judgment, and it'll come right out of his paycheck. Don't worry about that part, Josh." She hesitated. "Will you come back?"

"I thought you couldn't control me?"

"Oh, Josh. I'm confused. I'm sorry, honey. Come back. I need you." His mother sounded almost out of breath. "Laurel wants you here, Josh. She misses you. I do too."

"How?" Josh paced the brick walkway, one hand still clenching his hair, the other pressing the phone to his ear.

"That's my boy, Josh." He could feel his mom's relief. "Your father can take you to the airport and get you a ticket. He will. He has to. He can't take you out of state unless I agree, and I'm taking back my agreement."

"You can do that?"

"Josh, the bank put up a sign on the fence. They're going to auction our home. I can do whatever I have to do to stop it. I will do whatever I have to." Her voice turned mean, and Josh quaked at the thought of telling his father he wanted to go back. He'd never felt so torn in his life.

"Can I just go?" Josh said.

"What do you mean, honey?" his mother asked.

"He's gonna be mad, Mom."

"You let me talk to him, Josh. He'll behave."

Josh looked back at the dorm building. Hidden in the bushes beneath its ground-floor windows, a dozen spotlights lit the bricks and the painted white trim. It was enormous and solid, like a fortress. Josh just wanted to run. He felt more and more tied up, like a fishing line twisted and looped and knotted beyond repair.

"I don't know." His voice sounded distant. The shaggy tree above swallowed everything but the sound of the crickets.

"Just come home, Josh. You'll be able to sort things out better here."

"If I want to come back to Florida, can I?" Josh didn't want to cut off any escape routes, and he thought his father might let him leave more easily if there was a chance he might return.

"Of course," his mom answered, almost too fast. "If your father is willing to make the house payments and you feel like it's the best thing for you, Josh, I won't keep you from doing that. I won't want you to go, but I won't stop you. Just come back. I know you'll feel better with Jaden and Benji to talk to."

Josh almost asked his mother how she knew that's

what he'd been thinking but stopped himself. He had to be careful. With the state his parents were in, Josh needed to keep his cards close to the vest and play them very carefully. Hadn't his dad just said that he was glad Josh ran away? Now he knew why. This was getting really crazy.

"Okay. Dad might let me go then."

"Josh, he *has* to let you go. The police will take you if he doesn't."

"Police?"

"It's not going to happen. He won't let it. He *can't*. He's got this new, precious job. He can't afford to have trouble before he even gets started. Trust me."

"Okay." The thought of his friends, his home, his school, and his baseball team was too much. "But you gotta do it. Not me. I'm not telling him. I'll just go along. Okay? Can you do that?"

"Yes, as long as you want to come, I'll tell him he has to send you home. I'll take the heat."

"Should I just go back inside?" Josh asked.

"Yes. You can tell him as much or as little as you like. You can tell him to call me, or I'll just ring him up myself. Do you want me to wait and do it when you're there, or should I call now? Where are you?"

"Just outside, on a bench, under some trees."

"It's your call," she said.

"Okay," he said, "let me go back in. I'll tell him you were saying some stuff, but I didn't understand and I told you to talk to him about it."

"I'll give you ten minutes," she said. "I love you, Josh."

"I love you too, Mom." Josh hung up. He spent a few more minutes walking outside, thinking, before returning to the dorm room. It had only been a few days, and his whole life had fallen apart. And now, just when things were starting to settle down here in Florida, his house was being sold. He thought back to that home run derby. Maybe when he got back to Syracuse, he could still do it.

His father lay in the bed propped up on his pillow, working on his laptop. He looked over the tops of his glasses. "Feel better?"

Josh sat on the bed and focused on untying his shoes. "I don't know. I talked to Mom. She was talking kind of crazy. I'm not sure what she was even saying."

"Crazy, like what?" His father set his laptop down and sat up straight.

Josh shrugged.

His father's phone rang. He answered. "Laura? What's going on?"

Josh held his breath.

CHAPTER TWENTY-SEVEN

IT WASN'T EASY, BUT it wasn't as hard as Josh worried it might be. Whatever his mom said, his father kept his cool. He answered with a lot of low yeses and nos. It was as if his mom had everything all mapped out, and she simply boxed his dad into some kind of corner.

When he hung up, Josh winced, waiting for fireworks.

His father took a deep, deep breath, then let it out slow. "Josh, I'm sorry about all this. I really am, but it looks like you've got to go back. You'll be able to visit me. That's a good thing."

Josh looked across the small room into his father's eyes and knew that whatever she said, his mother hadn't given him away.

"I'll do what you guys need me to do." Josh spoke

quietly, almost in a whisper.

His father lay back and shut off the light. "Get some sleep, Josh. Tomorrow I'm taking you to the airport."

He couldn't help asking himself over and over why life couldn't just go back to what it had been before. He remembered all the fights his parents had. He thought nothing could be worse.

He'd been wrong.

The red numbers on the clock blinked 12:41 a.m. at him. No way did Josh think he'd ever sleep, but he did. He was exhausted, not from the baseball practice, but from worry and fright and sadness and confusion.

In the morning, his dad's sour face confirmed that the whole thing hadn't been a dream.

Although his flight wouldn't take off for a few hours, Josh stood waiting with his duffel bag until his father finished dressing and said, "Let's go." His dad was gruff, but without being mean. "Don't forget your base-ball stuff."

Josh had forgotten his equipment bag, maybe kind of on purpose. As he hoisted the bag, the bats clattered softly inside, making Josh remember the hundreds of practices he'd had with his dad over the past five years. That would now end, and he and his father looked at each other over the sound, both of them knowing. His dad threw his chin toward the front door and left the room.

Josh followed.

They listened to the satellite radio's classic rock station all the way to Orlando airport. After parking the car, Josh's dad went in with him, bought a ticket, checked his bags, and waited in the security line. Families with little kids sported mouse ears, princess wands, and duck lips. There was only a gray-haired couple left in front of them when Josh's father spoke.

"You seem pretty okay with all this."

Josh shrugged, wondering why the woman couldn't get the handle down into her mini suitcase. "I didn't know I had a choice."

His father looked at him sharply, then frowned. "I guess not. You'll come visit. Or . . . who knows?"

"Yeah," Josh said, "who knows?"

The older couple finally made it through. Josh heaved his backpack onto the belt and turned. His father hugged him, tighter than Josh could ever remember. "You be safe now, and take care of your little sister."

None of it even seemed real to Josh. A man with three little girls bumped into Josh's dad as he laid a stroller on the belt, breaking up their hug.

"Oh. Sorry," said the man.

"No, that's fine." Josh's dad turned back to Josh. "I love you, buddy."

"I love you too, Dad."

Josh turned and escaped through the metal detector. He got his backpack and headed for the tram to Gate

A. Before he turned the corner, he looked back. His dad stood like a giant, towering over the Disney tourists, serious and frozen, with something that might have been a tear traveling down his face.

Josh waved quickly and bolted for the closing doors of the tram.

He spent the next couple of hours reading his book and waiting until his plane was going to take off. Finally he boarded his direct flight, and a few hours later his mom picked him up in a borrowed car. She squeezed him and whispered, "I missed you." Laurel squealed with delight and buried her face in his chest as he hugged her to him. They didn't talk much on the short ride home. Laurel filled the silence, babbling with delight.

Josh climbed the stairs, and it seemed a longer climb than usual. He set his trophy carefully back on the dresser top and unpacked the rest of his bag as the sounds of Laurel getting ready for bed pierced the thin walls. Josh used the bathroom while his mom read to his sister, then bumped his head getting into bed. His mom came in and sat on the edge of his bed in the dark, reaching for Josh's hand and holding it tight.

For some unknown reason, Josh began to cry, comfortable doing so in the darkness with only his mom there.

"Why are you crying, Josh?" his mom asked.

He took several breaths before the words would come

out. "I . . . I . . . I just want us to be back to the way it was before."

She was quiet for some time before she smoothed his hair and sighed. "I know, Josh. But everything changes. That's just life. And sometimes, when you expect it least, tomorrow turns out to be a better day."

CHAPTER TWENTY-EIGHT

"**DUDE, YOU WERE BARELY** gone." Benji bit into his chocolate ice cream cone like it was an apple and chewed the same way.

Jaden spun her cone, cleaning up the edge of her vanilla. "I'm glad you're back. What's up with the house?"

Josh sat atop his bicycle, using one hand to balance against a chain-link fence and the other to tuck the last bit of his cone into his mouth. He crunched it down and swallowed. "Touch and go."

"Touch and go?" Benji swiped at the chocolate goo dribbling down his chin. "That sounds bad. Last touch and go I saw was my dad's job at the engine plant. 'Touch and go,' he'd said. More like touch and going, going, *gone.*"

"That has nothing to do with this." Jaden scowled and swatted at him. The two of them sat on a picnic bench at Kustard King. Their bikes rested on stands beside the fence. The AC unit atop the building hummed its sound.

"Everything has to do with everything." Benji swatted her right back. "Haven't you ever heard of Einstein's theories, you wannabe brainiac?"

"Just what theory are you talking about?" Jaden made a face, and Josh held back a laugh. Sometimes he was sure they enjoyed fighting.

"The one about relatives." Benji jutted out his chin. "It's, like, everyone's related. Like six degrees of relatives. Everyone on the whole planet. That means everything has to do with everything. It's like one of those sayings . . . a motto . . . a slogan or something."

"You are just so mixed up." Jaden looked at him sadly and licked her ice cream.

"Josh knows what I mean, don't you, Josh?"

Josh looked up at the sun and blinked. He took a deep breath. It was warm, but bakery warm, not swamp-sizzling, sweat-monster warm like Florida. "I'm not sure, Benji, but I can't focus. I keep thinking about that contest."

"Her contest?" Benji jagged a thumb toward Jaden.

"No, the home run contest," Josh said. "Winning a house. I mean, if that's for real, it could solve a lot of my problems. What contest is Jaden in anyway?"

"It's the Young Journalist Award," Jaden said. "You have to write a compelling story and get it published by November first to qualify. Then you just submit it and they pick the best one on November fifteenth, and you get a ten-thousand-dollar scholarship."

"Which is less likely than hitting a ball into a bathtub, I can tell you that," Benji said.

"Well, even if you're right about this so-called home run derby, if it has to *stay* in the tub, that's probably not even possible." Jaden took a bit of ice cream. "On the other hand, someone *will* win the Young Journalist Award, and if I can get a good enough idea, there's no reason it shouldn't be me. I need something original, that's all. And since I've already gotten some stories into the sports page at the *Post-Standard*, it probably should be something sports related. Maybe someone overcoming some incredible injury? Something like when you played with that cracked bone in your face. I'm just saying, Josh, if you get an idea."

"And if I get an idea?" Benji said.

"I think a baseball landing in a bathtub is more likely than you getting an original idea," Jaden said.

Benji's face turned red, but before he could hurl an insult, Josh cut him off. "It's good to be home; that's all I know."

"You miss your dad, though, I bet." Jaden tilted her head at him.

"Sure, but he's gotta be on the road all the time," Josh said. "What's that about?"

"College sports is serious stuff." Benji's words were barely understandable.

"Benji?" Jaden smiled warmly at him. "Anyone ever mention to you that you shouldn't talk with *food* in your mouth?"

Benji jammed the rest of his cone into his mouth and crunched, ending with a loud gulp.

"There, now my mouth is empty." Benji stuck out his tongue. "Now I can talk in the presence of Your Highness . . . and I'm telling you to slap a clapper on your piehole."

"I hate to say it, but I actually missed you two," Josh said.

"Heavy hitters are like Siamese twins, dude," Benji said. "You don't just separate them. Bad things happen."

Josh looked at his phone and saw the time. "Come on. We gotta get home and change. I don't want to be late to meet this new coach."

"Yeah." Jaden hopped down and climbed up on her bike. "From everything I've heard, you do not want to be late for Aaron Swanson."

"Oh, boy." Josh started to pedal.

"Dude, wait up!" Benji dusted his hands and got on his bike too. "He's not gonna mind if the heavy hitters show up fashionably late. We gotta let this Coach Swanson know who's running the show."

"Are you serious?" Josh shot a glance back over his shoulder at Benji.

CHAPTER TWENTY-NINE

"KIND OF." BENJI SOUNDED disappointed that Josh wasn't going along with him.

"Well, I for one am going to be on time." Josh downshifted gears and raised his butt up off his seat to climb the hill on Sixth North Street. "I just hope this Aaron Swanson guy can do it. Get us some wins, I mean. The scouts don't see you if you're not in the championship games."

"He took his last Little League team to the state finals," Jaden said, huffing.

"Finals?" Benji said. "We blew through the finals, and we had a car dealer for a coach, not even Josh's dad. Little League is nothing to get excited about. Any justice in the world, we woulda won the whole World Series. That screwball Marcus."

"You can't blame it on one person. C'mon, let's leave that one alone." Josh didn't want to start talking about Diane and her son. "Let's look ahead."

"Hey, take a right. Enough of this hill," Benji huffed, turning without them.

"Uh-uh." Josh shook his head and kept going.

"Why? C'mon!" Benji stopped his bike and howled. "What? You're afraid of going by Bricktown?"

"He's just being smart, Lido," Jaden said, drafting behind Josh. "You should try it sometime."

Benji muttered, but he got back up on his bike, chugged hard, and caught up with them. "I'm not afraid of Bricktown or anyone in it."

"You gotta have brains to be afraid," Jaden said.

"Who says? That English teacher? Mrs. Ribble? Ribble Fribble Bibble Dribble. That's what I call her," Benji said.

"She's helping me with my Young Journalist Award submission, so you better watch your own piehole before I stuff it with a sock," Jaden said. "Or a rock."

Josh just kept pedaling. "So, you need an idea?"

"It can be published from September first right up until November first," she said, "but every time I get something I think is going to be good, it just fizzles. I started to write about this linebacker from Fowler High School who walked onto the SU football team and now he's leading the ACC in tackles, but things like that have happened before. I need a juicy story. That's what

I need. I mean, a scholarship for *ten grand.*"

Benji could only whistle at that.

Josh gave Jaden a wink. No matter how much she carried on, money wasn't what it was about. She wanted the recognition this award would bring. Ever since he'd known her, Jaden had been working to become a Pulitzer Prize–winning reporter.

The sun was low in the sky. The tree-lined streets were busy with people returning home from work. Two kids sailed paper airplanes out the second-story window of their house as a big dog barked like a banshee down below, spinning in a frenzy of excitement. Josh sighed with contentment. This was exactly where he belonged.

They dropped Benji off first. Josh came next.

"Want me to ride you home?" He slowed his pedaling and wavered just before his driveway.

"No. Thanks. You better get your stuff together," Jaden said. "I'm serious about this Coach Swanson. He's hard-core. Everyone says so. Used to be in the marines. I heard he was wounded in Iraq . . . or Afghanistan."

"Are you serious?"

Jaden shrugged. "Who knows? You know how people like to talk."

"Well, see you in a few." Josh turned into his driveway and hopped down off his bike. He watched her ride until she disappeared around the corner, then put his bike in the detached garage. His father's old car, a gray

Taurus, sat hunched over a flat rear tire. His mom now took the bus to work, and Josh was dependent on other people's parents for rides, mostly Mrs. Lido. Even though she seemed happy to do it, Josh wished his mom would get the tire fixed. When he brought it up, his mom would only say that taking the bus saved her gas money. Josh hated talk like that, and he looked forward to the day he signed his first big baseball deal. It would be the last time anyone in his family talked about money, that was for sure.

He marched into the house, intent on getting his stuff together so as not to make Mrs. Lido and Benji wait for a single second. Then he saw his mom's face.

Black eyeliner smudged the skin beneath her eyes, giving her a raccoon-like appearance. Rubbing had left the whites of her eyes pink and red. She sat staring at the mug of coffee before her on the kitchen table, but when he said "Mom?" she looked up in horror.

"Well," she said, her face crumpling, "people always say that when it rains it pours."

Josh reached out to touch her shoulder. "What happened? What's wrong?"

CHAPTER THIRTY

HER EYES SHONE AT him with pain. "I lost my job, Josh."

"Mom?" Josh knew it was bad, even without the details.

"Belly up," she said. "They shut the whole business down. Janice's husband cleaned out their bank account and disappeared. I should feel bad for her, but I feel so bad for me and us that I . . ."

His mom started to cry, shaking from the effort of trying to hold it back. "I'm sorry."

"Oh, Mom." Josh hugged her tight. He could hear his sister in the other room, watching a Barney DVD on the TV. Once those DVDs had belonged to Josh, so he knew the words before they were even spoken. Barney was always laughing, always happy and wanting everyone else to be that way too.

After a few minutes, his mom gently pushed him away. "Okay, thanks. I'm okay now. Really. Don't you worry. Everything will be fine."

She got up and began pulling things from the cupboard: flour, baking powder, raisins, cinnamon, and oatmeal. She sniffed and opened the fridge. "Hope I have enough butter. Don't you have to get ready for practice? I thought we'd eat late tonight. I'm going to make some cookies, but can I fix anything to hold you over?"

Josh was relieved to have something else to think about, to worry about, even if choosing a snack couldn't stop the total meltdown of his family.

"A ham sandwich?" he asked.

"I'm an expert at ham sandwiches." She smiled and set the butter down and reached into the fridge again. "Cheese?"

"Yes, please." Josh ran upstairs for his glove, then retrieved his baseball cleats from the shoe rack and took down his equipment bag from its hook. "Jaden says this coach is hard-core. That he won a medal in Afghanistan."

"*What?*" His mom spun around with a butter knife in her hand.

"I mean," Josh said, "he was a soldier. He's supposed to be hard-core. I guess we're lucky the team got someone so quick, right?"

His mom finished slathering two slices of white

bread with mayonnaise. "There're plenty of people who want to coach the Titans. I give your father credit for that. It's a franchise. I heard the board had two dozen applications."

"I'm surprised they didn't give it to Coach Moose. Everyone loves him." Josh was so glad not to be talking about his mom losing her job that the words just spilled silly from his lips.

His mom tossed some ham slices on the bread, then peeled a piece of cheese off the slab she'd taken from the fridge. "He didn't want it."

"Why?" Josh asked.

His mom looked at him. "Some people don't want to be the focus of attention. Coach Moose likes being an assistant."

Josh processed that quickly, knowing that somewhere in her words was a trap having to do with his father, so he simply said, "Oh."

"Sit," his mom said. "You've got a minute."

Josh sat at the kitchen table.

"I knew Coach Swanson had served in the military." His mom put the sandwich together and slapped it down on the table atop a napkin. "That doesn't mean he's going to be unreasonably tough."

"What if he is?" Josh scooped up the sandwich and took a bite.

"Whatever he's like, he protected our country." She poured him a glass of milk and set that down. "So we owe him our thanks, and you should give him every chance before you jump to conclusions."

Josh digested that as he chewed. A horn honked from the driveway. He jumped up and kissed his mom and made for the door with the half-eaten sandwich in his hand. When he got into the car, Benji spun around in the front seat and looked at the sandwich with interest.

"Want some?" Josh offered what amounted to two remaining bites.

"If you're not gonna eat it," Benji said, reaching for it.

"Sure," Josh said.

"Benji, you ate two peanut butter and jellies at home." Benji's mom shook her head, and the big pile of blond hair stacked on top of her head wavered like a Jell-O mold.

"This is *ham*, Mom." Benji stuffed it into his mouth but kept talking. "Animal protein. It's the food of heavy hitters."

Benji's mom squeezed her lips tight. "Ham's expensive, Benji, but we do all right."

Benji grinned and winked at Josh.

Josh's stomach sank. He couldn't worry about not having ham. His family might not even have a house.

CHAPTER THIRTY-ONE

JOSH MADE ROOM FOR Jaden in the backseat. He'd taken it as a good sign that Coach Swanson kept Jaden on the team email list. He hoped it wasn't just an oversight and that the coach really wanted Jaden to continue to record stats for the team. Josh hoped the new coach would keep everything the same as it had been under his dad but knew that some things were bound to change. Not many coaches had a background in baseball like Josh's father.

"Hey, Benji," Josh said as they neared the school parking lot. "That contest you were talking about? What was the name of that company? I want to look that up online later."

Benji spun around. "Don't you believe me?"

"Of course," Josh said. "I just want to read the rules

about how you qualify and the stuff about the bathtub and make sure this thing is for real."

"You can win that thing, dude. I'm telling you." Benji nodded vigorously. "Yeah, it's as real as the nose on my face."

Jaden reached out and tugged his nose. "Yup, that's real."

"Dude!" Benji swatted her away. "Don't touch the merchandise! You don't just walk into a museum and start touching things."

"Museum? We're in your mom's car," Jaden said.

"Yeah, but this is fine art." Benji pointed to his nose. "Like the *Mona Lisa* or that *David* statue."

"How many dingers do you have to hit during fall ball to qualify?" Josh asked as they headed to the field, his mind again on the contest.

"Dude, twenty, but you can do that," Benji said. "We play like thirty games this fall. That's nothing for you, blasting twenty round-trippers."

"It's not nothing," Jaden said.

"How would you know?"

"I keep the stats, right?" she said. "Now you're gonna tell me about the stats, Mr. Mona Lisa?"

"You're gonna tell me Josh can't do this?" Benji held out his traffic cop hand. "You wanna talk to the hand for the rest of the day today?"

"I'm not saying he can't." Jaden slapped Benji's hand away. "He can, but it's not going to be easy. Even if he hits as well as he did all summer, it'll be close. Every game will count. Every home run."

"Heavy hitters play that way no matter what. You already know that if you're half as smart as you think you are." Benji turned around, ending the conversation.

When they arrived at the ball field, Esch and Lockhart gave them high fives. Josh could already see Coach Swanson standing at home plate with his arms folded across his broad chest. He had a crew cut that didn't hide the three-inch white scar on the right side of his skull. He was wiry and not very tall, but he kept his back ramrod straight. He watched the team, his team, without speaking as they unloaded their equipment bags, slipped on their gloves, and began to form a small half circle beneath his iron gaze.

Josh and Benji dumped their stuff in the dugout, and Josh leaned close to Benji. "Glad you didn't arrive fashionably late now?"

"Holy moly." Benji's eyes were frozen on their new coach as he whispered, "You see that scar?"

"How could you miss it?" Josh felt a thrill of excitement, not about the new coach, but just about being back with the guys he knew on a field he'd practiced on for months in weather that was warm without being a steam bath.

He fist-bumped with Paul Goldfarb, their rangy third baseman who hustled out of the dugout.

"You think it was a bullet or a knife?" Benji

whispered, still stuck on the new coach's scar.

"Why don't you ask him?" Josh stepped out of the dugout.

Benji hustled and caught up to him. "Did you leave your brains in Disney World?"

Josh said nothing because they were in the circle of players now and Coach Swanson was pointing to him. "You're LeBlanc."

It wasn't a question, but Josh nodded his head anyway, and he couldn't help thinking how nice it'd been when his father was the coach. Josh had nothing to prove with his father, nothing to worry about. All he had to do was work hard and his father would be pleased. With this coach Josh didn't know.

"Thought we weren't going to have you this season," Coach Swanson said. "Florida or something?"

Josh shrugged.

"Well, I'm darn glad you're here."

The coach sounded like he meant it, but Josh couldn't read his eyes.

The coach turned them on Benji. "You Lido?"

"Heavy hitter two, Coach." Benji's words lacked their usual conviction.

Coach Swanson frowned and looked Benji up and down. "You're heavy, that I won't argue with. And you must be Jaden Neidermeyer. Glad you're on with us."

Coach Swanson made a note on his clipboard. "I like the articles you've written about the team. I'm hoping you can keep that going."

Jaden blushed. "Well, it'll be harder to get articles in for fall ball. People want to read about football."

"My money's on you." Coach Swanson smiled at Jaden before directing his attention back to Josh. "Your father was smart, more than just a good coach. He sold this team, great public relations, all that. Nike doesn't sponsor just anyone, you know. There are only five Nike travel teams in the country, so you not only have to win, people have to notice."

"Thanks." Josh thought of his father down at Crosby College, sweating and working in the heat. A shiver of guilt scurried up his spine.

"Did you ever help with the paperwork, Jaden?" Coach Swanson held up a folder stuffed with papers. "I've got these tournament applications. I've already made copies of everyone's birth certificates. No pressure, but if you're going to be around, I've got lots for you to do."

Josh recognized the folder as the same one his father had used. He knew coaching the Titans came with a lot of paperwork. The tournaments they played in always required every player to be registered and to prove that he was eligible.

"Sure, Coach. I'm happy to help." Jaden took the folder from him.

"So, gentlemen," Coach Swanson said, addressing the whole team before he bowed to Jaden, "and one lady. This is the Nike-sponsored Syracuse Titans. I am Coach Swanson. We have five days to get to know one another before we head out to Cambridge for the Harvard Classic, the first of eight tournaments over the next two months. During that time we will distinguish ourselves as the best U13 fall ball team in the land. We will practice outside unless it looks like rain or it gets too cold, then we will be inside the Mount Olympus Sports Complex just as you've been in the past.

"Now, let's get something straight. I am not Coach LeBlanc. As much as I respect Coach LeBlanc and everything he did with this team, this will be the last time we talk about him. You belong to me now. I will be demanding. We will do things my way now, whether you like it or not, and you will not question me. Do not tell me how things were done in the past; only do as I ask in the future. We are here to win. Is that understood?"

Coach Swanson glared around at them. "Is that understood?"

"Yes!" They barked like a pack of dogs, answering his growl.

"Good." Coach Swanson nodded and pointed toward the visiting team's empty dugout, and a skinny boy with crooked glasses, a crutch, and leg braces limped toward them as if he were drawn to Coach Swanson's finger by a string. "This is Martin Sheridan. He's like family to me. He's our manager. He won't replace you,

Miss Neidermeyer, but Martin will be my right hand."

Martin's hardware clattered in the silence. He gave his hips a final swing, came to a halt, and hung his head. A curtain of brown hair hid his downturned face.

"Look up, Martin!" Coach Swanson's bark startled the team.

Martin forced his chin up and revealed big, dark eyes and a pale face.

"Martin has moderate cerebral palsy, but that doesn't slow him down." Coach Swanson's voice was hard. "He doesn't feel sorry for himself, and you're not to feel sorry for him, either. If he asks you for something, it's like I'm asking you for something, so you'll do it."

The look on Martin's face suggested Josh's little sister, Laurel, was tougher, but like the rest of them, he said nothing.

"Also, Coach Moose." Coach Swanson looked at his clipboard. "He will be with us, but not for the next two days, because he's at some teachers' conference. Finally, we are missing one player—Martin's older brother. His name is Jack Sheridan, and he will be here for tomorrow's practice. He's from North Carolina, and he'll be our ace—our go-to pitcher."

A gasp rumbled through the team. Kerry Eschelman had been the team's number-one pitcher since Josh's dad formed the Titans U12 team last spring. Esch had a wicked arm and had won the team plenty of games, including a national championship at Cooperstown. He had also developed into a potent hitter with Josh's dad's coaching.

Gary Lockhart stepped forward as if to say something. Their left fielder had a strong arm but not much of a bat.

"Oh? Some of you don't like that?" Coach Swanson's smile seemed wicked. "Trust me, when you see Jack pitch, you won't be disappointed. Esch, there'll be plenty of work for you too; you know that."

Esch's freckled face had reddened at the attention. He was a quiet kid anyway, and all he did was nod to the coach.

"I presume everyone here has a cell phone?" Coach Swanson looked around.

Everyone nodded.

"Right." Coach Swanson nodded to Martin, who adjusted a duffel bag he had slung across his shoulders, opening it for them to fill. "Put your cell phones in Martin's bag. That's where they go at the beginning of every practice and every game. No distractions. We're here to work, not text our girlfriends."

A few of the players twittered at that, and Billy Duncan burst out with a laugh he cut short.

"You'll get them back at the end of every practice, so there's no need to worry." Coach Swanson then blasted his whistle. "Okay! Dump your gloves in the on-deck circle. Form a line behind home plate. This team is going to get in shape. People think baseball is relaxed and casual. Not my team. We'll never phone it in: we work hard, we train hard, and we play as hard in the last inning of the last game as we do in the first. On my whistle you jog down the first-base line, around the inside of the fence, back down the third-base line, then sprint around the bases and do it all over again. Six times. We gotta run fast when we're tired. If you can pass someone, do it. I will be watching to see who lags and who wants to win. Ready? One at a time, on my whistle."

Josh had jumped and was first in line at home plate. Coach blasted his whistle, and Josh took off at a steady jog, circling the field. When he hit home plate, he burst around the bases and set out again. Josh passed Benji on the second lap and Lockhart and Duncan soon after. Martin leaned on his crutch and remained at Coach Swanson's side. After the sixth lap the coach told Josh to get some water. Josh threw himself down on the bench beside Jaden and sucked down half the water in his bottle.

Jaden was completing some paperwork for the Harvard Classic. "Not like the old days, huh?"

"What's he think we've got next weekend, a baseball tournament or a marathon?" Josh gasped for breath.

"That which doesn't kill you . . . ," Jaden said.

"Makes you stronger, I know." Josh slapped his knees and got up. "But if we do too much of this junk, someone will get killed."

Jaden looked out at the field and Benji's big, wobbly shape as he struggled along the outfield fence. "Meaning Benji?"

"I just don't know how much of this stuff the big guy can take."

"What if he really can't make it?" Jaden asked.

Josh glanced at Coach Swanson, standing like a statue behind home plate, checking off kids as they crossed home plate for the final lap.

Josh bit his lower lip. "I'd hate to find out, but I think we're about to."

CHAPTER THIRTY-TWO

JOSH HEADED OUT TO home plate to cheer on the stragglers. He high-fived the guys as they stumbled across home plate and headed to the dugout for some more water. Josh didn't look at Coach Swanson or Martin. He just did his thing the way his father had taught him, encouraging the guys, even Billy Duncan, who came in second to last, and then Benji, who still had a final lap to go even after Duncan had finished.

Josh patted Benji's butt. "C'mon, Benji. Do it, buddy!"

Benji stopped and turned the saddest eyes he could muster on their new coach. "Coach, can I call it with everybody else?"

Benji could barely speak, and he sounded like he was about to cry. His dark hair was plastered to his forehead. Sweat poured from his face and dripped from his ears.

"Man up, Lido. This isn't kindergarten. Everybody doesn't get a medal for trying. Finish!" Coach Swanson shouted, pointing a finger down the first-base line.

As Benji slogged off, Coach Swanson blew his whistle again. "Let's go, long toss. Partner up on the first-base line!"

"What about Benji, Coach?" Josh asked.

Coach Swanson watched with disgust as Benji waddled across first base and kept going. "What about him?"

"Well, my d—" Josh caught himself and stopped before he quoted his father about how a team sticks together. Coach Swanson glared at Josh and looked like his head might explode.

"My . . . my darn cleats," Josh said, thinking fast. "Too tight, Coach. Gotta get a new pair."

"What's that got to do with Lido?"

Josh shrugged. "Maybe he's got the same problem?"

"Long toss, LeBlanc. You leave Lido to me."

Josh nodded, got his glove, and paired off with Preston to warm up their arms with a long toss. As they threw, Josh kept his eyes on Benji, silently urging him to make it. Josh was beyond third base when Benji passed him, chugging as slow as cold honey, gasping and heading for home. Just before the plate, Benji went down. He collapsed slowly, melting rather than falling,

146

and his chin ended up on the rubber. Josh stopped his throwing and moved toward his friend.

"I made it, Coach." Benji barked like a wounded seal, looked up at the coach with a painful smile, then barfed all over home plate.

CHAPTER THIRTY-THREE

"LIDO!" COACH SWANSON HOWLED. "You get that mess off of home plate!"

Benji rolled over on his back and flopped his arms out to the sides. "I can't move, Coach. I can't move. Aw, the ham and cheese . . . gone."

"Clean that up, Lido." The coach glowered at the puke. "Get some cardboard and the rake from the equipment shed to clear it. You're gonna need some fresh dirt. Before you're done, douse the plate with water—and get yourself cleaned up too."

Coach Swanson stomped off to the outfield. He marched around the grass and kept a surprisingly watchful eye on the team, barking out commands sometimes to the players right in front of him or sometimes to the ones halfway across the field.

Josh kept stealing glances at Benji as he struggled with the infield rake and shoveled the mess onto a piece of wet cardboard. Dejectedly, he dumped it in a garbage barrel before raking some fresh dirt into the ground.

Swanson barked, "Lido, now water it down!"

Benji staggered back from the bathroom, struggling with both hands to control the sloshing water in the bucket. He finally made it to home plate and doused it with the water.

"Get to work, Lido!" the coach shouted. "Put that bucket back and come out here!"

Benji stalked off with the bucket and got his glove. Halfway to the outfield he shouted, "Where you want me, Coach?" as if nothing was amiss.

"Shag balls with LeBlanc and Zigmansky!"

"Are you okay?" Josh whispered at Benji when he arrived.

"You two!" Coach Swanson shouted from two drills away. "Stop talking gumdrops and lollipops and get to work!"

"I'll give him a gumdrop," Benji muttered beneath his breath.

"What's that, Lido?" Coach Swanson headed their way with his hands on his hips and shouting like he meant it. "You got something to say, or is that just more barf leaking from your piehole?"

"Nothing, Coach!" Benji shouted, scowling at Josh like it was his fault.

Josh didn't know if it was because Benji made a mess on home plate or if every practice was going to be as brutal, but brutal it was. They worked nonstop for two hours and ended with baseline sprints, and Benji catching a tongue lashing for lagging behind. Finally, the coach brought them in and answered Josh's question.

"Well, I took it easy on you tonight, but we're going to have to work a lot harder if we want to sweep this season." Coach Swanson stared around at them all as if daring someone to deny that they were going to win every single game they played. "That's how you gotta look at it, men. You gotta believe you're gonna win every time you walk onto that field. The ones who don't? You'll weed yourselves out. I've seen it before. Now bring it in for a break.

"'No guts, no glory'—that's our chant. Let me hear it on three! One, two, three!"

"NO GUTS, NO GLORY!" they all shouted, even Martin.

"All right," Coach Swanson said, "everyone take two handouts from Martin. One has his email and cell phone info. The other asks for your information. Fill it out carefully. If you're old enough to play for the Syracuse Titans U13 Travel Team, you are old enough to be responsible for yourselves. All practice announcements and team business will be emailed and/or texted to you and your parents by Martin. If this doesn't work for you or your parents, good luck finding another team. I'll give you a glowing recommendation."

Josh took a handout from Martin. "Hey, thanks, Martin."

Martin didn't even look up but handed a paper to Benji.

Josh let the others drain into the parking lot before he doubled back to speak with Coach Swanson. Martin was in the dugout, struggling with a latch on the equipment bag. Josh went to help him, but Martin just mumbled, "I got it." Josh sighed and let him alone.

Coach Swanson hadn't moved, and he looked up from his clipboard. "What can I do for you, LeBlanc?"

Josh cleared his throat; the cold look on his coach's face made him wish he hadn't come back. It was a bad thing to ask. It didn't have anything to do with winning. This wasn't Coach Moose or Josh's dad. This was an ex-soldier who'd probably killed people with his bare hands.

Josh opened his mouth and gurgled.

"Well?" Coach Swanson's thick eyebrows knit together above his nose. "I've got work here, LeBlanc. Spit it out."

CHAPTER THIRTY-FOUR

AN UNFRIENDLY VEIN APPEARED in Coach Swanson's forehead.

Josh began to sweat. "I . . . I just. It's nothing, really, Coach. I shouldn't have bothered you."

"Okay, but you did, so what's up?"

"It's just that Qwik-E-Builders Home Run Derby?"

Coach Swanson narrowed his eyes. "I'm not a gimmick guy, LeBlanc, if that's what you're asking. I see you got a big bat, but that contest is just a marketing ploy by some company to get people talking about it like you and I are doing right now. First you gotta qualify, and twenty home runs are a lot when we only play thirty-two games. Second, you gotta drop one of your home runs into a soup bowl or something."

"Yeah, but . . . I think it's a bathtub," Josh said. "Someone could win."

"And I could hit a ball from here to the moon."

Josh tried to read his coach's face. He had no idea where this craziness was headed.

"You don't think I'm really gonna do that, do you?" Coach Swanson spoke softly.

Josh shook his head.

"No," the coach said, then paused. "What do you want, LeBlanc?"

Josh did have something he wanted, but something about Coach Swanson's face had him all muddled. It was like they were on two different wavelengths. "Coach?"

"Why are you here?" Coach Swanson asked. "You must have something in mind. Everyone talked about you going down to Florida with your dad. What an amazing opportunity, your dad the college coach? Travel teams in the area probably crawling over each other to get you signed up, but here you are, with me. So I'm curious. It can't be trying to win a house."

Josh opened his mouth. It wasn't the reason he came back, but it was a good reason now. The real reason was embarrassing. "It's just my family."

"Hey." Coach Swanson held his hands up as if he were surrendering a weapon. "I get that. Personal. None of my business. It's all good, LeBlanc. I know lots of broken families. So . . ."

"I just wanted you to know that I'd be going for that thing," Josh said. "The house. That's all. Even if it's hard. I'm gonna try."

"Well, good. You do that. All set now?"

Josh wasn't set. He wanted to ask for something, a favor that just might help him win the house.

CHAPTER THIRTY-FIVE

JOSH KEPT HIS MOUTH shut, thinking. If he asked now and got a no, it would be over. It just didn't seem the right time or place to ask. He felt he had to trust his instincts. "Yes, I'm all set. Thanks, Coach."

"Hey. Any time."

Josh turned away, wondering why in the world he had thanked Coach Swanson. He hadn't even gotten to say what he wanted, let alone get it from his new coach. Josh took off at a jog to catch up to his friends.

"What was that about?" Benji asked. "Secret hand-shakes or something?"

"I wanted to see if he had any tips about switch-hitting." Josh could bat with either hand, and he knew any talk about switch-hitting impressed Benji enough to distract him from the real story.

"Yeah." Benji gave a knowing nod. "I gotta ask him that myself."

"Lido, you bat like James Bond from the other side of the plate," Jaden said.

"Bond?" Benji raised an eyebrow.

"Yeah, like 007. That'd be your average."

"Funny, wisenheimer. Real funny."

"Well, don't sweat it, big guy," Jaden said. "There aren't many people who *can* switch-hit like Josh. He's like Mark Teixeira, and how many of those guys are around?"

"I don't need to hear about your Yankee Tex." Benji held up a hand like he was stopping traffic. "It's Big Papi or bust for me. There are no other hitters."

"Here we go. . . ." Jaden rolled her eyes. They all knew Benji was a die-hard Red Sox fan.

When they were loaded into Benji's mom's car and under way, Josh looked back at the parking lot, where Martin was struggling to load the trunk of Coach Swanson's car. "I feel bad for that kid."

"No one deserves to be treated like that." Benji sat hunched over in the front seat, still grumpy thinking about the coach.

Benji's mom wrinkled her nose. "You smell like throw up."

"For a reason, Mom," Benji said, before turning to Josh and changing the subject back to Martin. "Don't feel too bad. You said thanks for the paper, and he didn't even give you a grunt. That's no way to behave, not in my house anyway, right, Mom?"

Mrs. Lido gave a big nod worthy of a woman with a son like Benji. "Saying 'you're welcome' is a *must*, Benji; you know that. I've always taught you."

"See?" Benji swung around to make sure Jaden was paying attention before turning back to his mom. "Manners can take you farther than brains, right, Mom?"

"Oh, I always say that, and you know it, Benji. Look at your uncle Mert. Lucky to get a C on his school report card, but the boy had manners out the ying-yang, and he's got a house in Hilton Head on the beach." Mrs. Lido glanced in the rearview mirror at Josh. "On the *beach*."

Jaden said nothing, but rolled her eyes and grinned at Josh as they rode on in silence.

At home, Josh's mom had already put Laurel to bed and was sitting with a book in the TV room.

"How'd it go?" she asked.

"Good." Josh sat and picked up the remote.

"Can we not have the noise, Josh?" his mom said. "It's been a long day."

"The Yankees are playing, Mom." He gave her a wounded look.

"Fine." She opened her book back up. "Keep the volume down."

Josh put the set on. Laurel had been watching a DVD. He switched the input and got nothing. He switched it around again before he got up and wiggled the cable in the box below the TV. "Mom, the cable's not working."

She looked up from her book, closing it, and bit her lower lip. "Oh. Uh, well, it may be off."

"Like someone hit the wire or something?" Josh asked.

"Well, Josh, honestly, I haven't paid that bill in some time. I don't really watch TV, and Laurel has her DVDs."

Josh didn't think before he spoke. "Yeah, but I gotta watch the Yankees. They're playing the Tigers."

Her spine went rigid. She pinched her lips and opened her book. "You 'gotta watch the Yankees'? You play enough baseball. I don't think you have to watch it too. I've had to make choices, Josh. Trust me; it hasn't been fun."

Josh felt a bit bad. "I get it, Mom. I know. I'm sorry. I'm just tired from practice. But you can turn it back on now, right? I mean, with me back, you're going to get the money you need from Dad. You said everything would be fine, right?"

CHAPTER THIRTY-SIX

HIS MOM SLAPPED THE book shut. Her face was grim.
"You coming back would have let us keep this house
if I didn't lose my job, Josh. I know you're a kid, but
I'm sorry—you're going to have to grow up fast. I can't
be worried about cable TV. I've got to feed us. I've got
to keep a roof over our heads. Honestly? If your father
hadn't already paid for fall ball, there is no way we'd be
able to afford it. I would never have wasted money on
something like *that*."

"Wasted?" Josh felt his blood heating up. "I'm going
to be a pro, Mom. It's an investment."

"Josh, please." She waved a hand and looked out the
window. "I've spent a lifetime watching that dream go
nowhere with your father. Let's not do it again with
you, okay?"

It was like a switch got flipped in his brain. All the crazy, ugly, nasty stuff between his mom and dad turning him into a human yo-yo, and now this? His mom trashing his dream jolted Josh. He jumped up and raised his voice. "Yeah, well not only am I gonna make it to the pros and buy you a Mercedes, I've got a chance to fix *everything* right now, thanks to fall ball!"

"What are you even talking about?" She looked like she'd eaten a lemon.

"I'm talking about the Qwik-E-Builders derby. I'm gonna win us a house, Mom. No more banks, no more bills, no more problems." Josh crossed his arms and nodded with pride.

She shook her head like he was crazy. "Josh, no one wins those things. They're a gimmick."

"That's not true, Mom. Benji says the FTC watches people so they can't just scam you like that." Josh tried not to let his voice falter, even though he realized he'd just quoted Benji.

"Okay, maybe it's *possible* to win, Josh," she said, "but no one actually does. You're talking about a *house*."

"It's a modular home company called Qwik-E-Builders." Josh threw his hands up in the air. "It's advertising for them. Coach says it's to get people talking like we're doing now, but I *could* win. I hit twenty home runs, I go to the derby in Houston. I get twenty pitches to win that thing, and if I dump one in this bathtub over the center-field fence, I win us a *house*."

His mom sighed and shook her head.

"Mom, listen. *Dad* got me ready for this thing. I know you're mad at him, but listen. How many of his pitches have I hit? Ten thousand? Ten million?"

"Not ten million," she said.

"Yeah, but you know what I mean. He taught me for the past six years how to hit a ball right, left, center, high, low, line drive. I've got the *bat* to do this."

"Oh, Josh. Come here." His mom reached out and pulled him to her. She pressed the side of her head against his stomach and hugged him tight. "You chase your dreams. Go ahead. But I've got to be practical. I called the bank. I can't keep lying and hiding and hoping the worst won't happen. I've got a place."

Josh pushed away. "What do you mean, you've got a place?"

Her lower lip crept beneath her teeth.

"An apartment. The broker came by while you were at practice. I signed the lease, and we can start getting moved in right away. I thought it'd be good before school starts."

"Apartment? Where?"

"On Woodrow Street." He could tell it took effort for her not to drop her chin. "It has a new stove."

"Mom, Woodrow?" Josh felt sick. "That's . . . that's borderline Bricktown."

CHAPTER THIRTY-SEVEN

JOSH COULDN'T SLEEP.

Over and over in his mind he replayed the conversation with his mom.

"But I came back so you wouldn't have to sell the house!" Josh said.

His mom nodded. "I know, honey. I didn't expect to lose my job and not even get my last month's paycheck. It was going to be tight as it was. Now it's impossible."

Josh clenched his teeth.

"Do you want to go back?" His mother spoke in the softest of whispers. "I'll understand if you do. I won't be mad."

"Back to Florida?" Josh's heart nearly stopped.

"Yes." His mother hung her head and wrinkled her mouth as if in pain.

"No, Mom," he said. "I'm not going back. I'm staying

with you and Laurel and my friends. This is where I belong."

At some point he did drop off to sleep, but the next day he was a zombie. His mom started packing things and didn't ask him to help. He felt guilty but couldn't stay. He had work to do. He gathered up Benji and Jaden on their bikes, and they rode out to the batting cages in North Syracuse.

Benji hit a few, but Josh was there for serious work. He swung until his arms were tired, blasting balls into the net with regularity.

Even Benji was impressed. "Heavy hitter."

Jaden nodded in agreement from her perch on the picnic table outside the cage where she'd been pecking away at her iPad, working on ideas for her Young Journalist Award submission. She was now torn between concussions and a new development in Tommy John surgery. "That was really great hitting, but I'm hungry just from watching you. Let's go have lunch."

"How about the mall?" Benji suggested.

They rode their bikes and sat in the food court. Jaden had some French fries while Benji knocked down two double cheeseburgers with a big shake. Even though the batting session had gone well, Josh just didn't have an appetite until he smelled their food. He went for a Whopper and wolfed it down.

"Good man," Benji said. "Us heavy hitters gotta keep our strength up."

They played hangman on Jaden's iPad, and Jaden tried to pick up Josh's spirits. "I know what I said, Josh, but if anyone could win that house, it's you. In the meantime, Woodrow Street isn't so bad. Besides, you know a girl at school who lives there. She's great. Shari Ann Harbaugh, you know her?"

"Yeah." Josh said, looking at the game. "But I heard her brother got beaten up by some gang called the Skulls."

"I said it when we were riding our bikes." Benji spoke through a mouthful of his chocolate shake. "You can't be afraid of Bricktown, or the Skulls, either. They put their pants on same as the rest of us."

"Things happen all over the city. You know that." Jaden entered a "T" for Josh in the hangman game, and the right arm of the stick figure appeared. Josh was dangerously close to being hung, only a hand away.

"My point is, that place is like a war zone. My dad would never go for something like that. Down in Florida, he got us this place with a pool and flower beds everywhere. He wasn't gonna put me in something like Bricktown."

"If you need protection, I'll come walk you to the bus stop when school starts." Benji snickered.

"That's not funny," Jaden grumbled to Benji, then turned to Josh. "Your mom doesn't have much of a choice, does she?"

"I have no idea," Josh said, looking at the game. "How about a 'B'?"

"Sorry." She entered the "B"; the hand appeared, hanging Josh's stick figure, turning his eyes to Xs and ending the game.

"That's about right." Josh looked sadly at the iPad. "What was it?"

"'Armadillo,'" Jaden said.

"Yeah, that was gonna be my next guess," Benji said.

"Right," Josh said. "Let's go."

They rode home, and Josh got changed for baseball. Benji's mom picked them up, the same as the night before. Jaden asked them if they remembered their information sheets.

"No. What are you, the Gestapo?" Benji asked, making his first WW II reference of the day.

"Just trying to help," she said.

"I got mine," Josh said. "Thanks."

When they arrived at the field, Josh picked the new kid out right away. He was atop the mound, throwing to Coach Swanson. It was all heat. The boy, Jack Sheridan, had everyone staring, even as they handed their information sheets to Martin. Josh glanced at Esch, who seemed unaffected, even though he must have known that his spot as top dog on the mound wouldn't be coming back anytime soon.

"That's your brother?" Josh handed Martin his sheet

and glanced toward the mound. The two of them looked nothing alike.

Martin took a glance at his brother. "Yeah, he looks like our dad."

Jack Sheridan had tan skin and brown hair cut close. He wore a look of angry concentration. Josh had the strangest feeling that he'd seen the kid before, but he had no idea where. He racked his brain but came up with nothing. Everyone watched the show, and Coach Swanson wasted the first ten minutes of their practice, ignoring everyone else so he could work with Sheridan.

Benji leaned close to Josh. "Kid's an animal. You believe that's Martin's *brother*?"

Josh shrugged.

Finally, Coach Swanson came up out of his crouch and blew his whistle.

"Guys, this is Jack Sheridan. Say hello."

Josh and everyone else murmured halfhearted greetings.

"Hey," said Jack Sheridan, looking around without much concern for the cool greeting. He wasn't as tall as Josh, but Sheridan had thick shoulders and a confident air. With his head tilted slightly back, he gave the impression of being the biggest kid among them. And as Josh looked at him, he wondered if he was older than thirteen. But before he could say anything to Benji or Jaden, Coach continued.

"Okay. Martin?" Coach Swanson looked around.

Martin made his way up to the group. "Sir?"

"You get everyone's text and email information?"

"Everyone but Lido, Coach."

"Lido?" Coach Swanson's face clouded over. "Why is that, Lido?"

"Oh yeah. Heck, Coach. I . . . well, my mom had all these jobs for me to do, and I kind of forgot."

"Jobs?"

"Yeah." Benji broke out in a sweat. "She's tough, my mom. Not as tough as my dad, but he's the top offensive lineman for the Syracuse—"

"Jobs that you worked on straight through the night? What jobs?" Coach wasn't going to let Benji off easy.

"Well . . . I had to feed the dog. Um . . . cut the grass and paint. I had to paint the garage. Yeah, that took forever, Coach."

"So, if I drive over to your house after practice to talk with your mom about how you didn't get your information in and ask her if you painted the garage the whole time you were home in the past twenty-two hours, she's gonna tell me that's true?" Coach Swanson glowered.

"I . . . uh. Well, I guess I *could* have gotten it done, Coach."

"Right. Okay, Lido. Start running."

"Coach?" Benji's face fell.

"Start running. Around this field, outside the fence. I'll tell you when you can stop." Coach Swanson tooted his whistle and pointed to the opening in the fence beside the dugout. "Go."

Benji glanced at Josh with a hopeful look. Josh just shook his head.

They began by warming up their arms and legs—Josh wasn't alone in being sore all over from the previous day's work—and the team moaned and groaned. Benji continued his slow slog around the field, even as practice wore on. When they worked on hitting, Gary Lockhart ended at bats with a weak grounder to second. Then Josh stepped up to the left side of the plate and banged every other pitch the rightie Esch threw him out of the park. Halfway through, he switched over to the right side and blasted them just as hard and often.

"Your bat looks darn good from both sides, LeBlanc." Coach Swanson almost sounded impressed. "Maybe you'll win that house yet."

Jack Sheridan was up after Josh, and when he handed him the bat, Sheridan muttered his thanks and stepped up to the plate. Josh got into position near second base and watched with surprise as Sheridan proceeded to hit every bit as well as Josh, even if it was only from one side of the plate. That was about the only bragging right Josh had left. Otherwise, Jack Sheridan was just as good a baseball player as Josh, if not better.

Meanwhile, Benji continued to jog. Halfway through practice, he stopped behind the backstop and gripped the fence like a caged animal. "Coach? Did you forget me?"

"No, Lido." Coach Swanson looked up from his

clipboard. "I like you right where you are. My bet is that next time you'll get your information in when you're supposed to without any problem at all. It's not fun to run the entire time, is it?"

"I gotta do this the whole practice?" Benji groaned. "Coach, come on. Have a heart. I'm one of your heavy hitters."

"I don't have a heart, Lido. I just want to win. Get your overloaded can moving. Now!"

Benji set off with a whimper. Josh felt bad for him, but, like the rest of the team, he cracked to it with whatever Coach Swanson had them doing. Practice ran like what Josh imagined boot camp in the army would be. They never stopped moving. The whistle never seemed to stop blowing.

Great at third baseman, Goldfarb was a slap hitter. He again showed the skill, drawing walks that put him near the top of the lineup.

After every pitch during batting practice, Coach insisted the infield and the outfield send the ball around the horn, keeping everyone on their toes and working their arms until Josh felt like his own might drop off.

Josh wanted to say something, but the sight of Benji circling the field and limping along now like a wounded elephant kept Josh from speaking his mind. He somehow knew that not only would it not do any good, but it wouldn't be tolerated.

After fifteen minutes of solid running, practice

finally ended. Coach Swanson called them all in. Benji dragged himself into the back of the group. Coach Swanson flashed a look of disgust at Benji and put his hand on Jack Sheridan's shoulder. "So, you've all seen what Jack can do. I wanted everyone to be clear so there's no whining or complaining. The fact is—and some of you may have figured this out already—we can only carry eighteen on our roster. Those are league rules. We've got our first tournament this coming weekend.

"Which means, with Jack joining us . . . someone has to go."

Josh looked over at Benji and felt a chill.

CHAPTER THIRTY-EIGHT

COACH SWANSON HAD THEM bring it in for their chant. "No guts, no glory" took on a new meaning for Josh. Fall ball without Benji knotted his stomach. As nutty as Benji could be, they really were like ice cream and cake. Josh didn't want to face fall ball—and the push for the home run derby—without him.

Benji was so upset, he began muttering in the dugout about having his parents call Nike to lodge a complaint about their new coach.

"Hey, your dad must know someone, right?" Benji asked Josh. "No way the new pitcher is thirteen."

Benji bent down to pick up his glove, and Josh saw that Sheridan was sitting at the end of the dugout, possibly listening. Josh tried to signal Benji to be quiet, but that was never easy.

"What? A call from your dad, and I bet we can end this guy's career with Nike. They don't like age cheats." Benji lowered his voice but not as much as Josh would have liked. Still, the new kid went about his business, and Josh felt like maybe he hadn't heard Benji.

They gathered their things and piled into Benji's mom's car.

"What's wrong, Benji?" Benji's mom put the car into gear and pulled away.

Benji shook his head. "I'm about ready to call Nike and have this guy fired."

Josh gave Jaden a look. She squeezed her lips tight.

"He's not a good coach?" Benji's mom was instantly concerned.

"He's terrible. He thinks baseball is the Boston Marathon. Baseball is baseball. To win, you throw the ball, catch it, and hit." Benji reached into his bag, pulled out a blue Gatorade, and chugged half of it down before stopping to burp. "Man, Josh, your dad really burned us."

"Well, he wanted to move up." Josh felt odd defending his dad, but he meant it.

"Yeah, but Swanson? He thinks he's still in the marines. And what about Bricktown?" Benji chugged the rest of his Gatorade and graced them with another loud burp. "You can't be loving that."

"What? Where did that come from? What does that have to do with baseball?" Suddenly, Josh didn't feel so bad for Benji. "Lots of people live there, Benji. Shari Ann Harbaugh lives there, and she's fine."

Benji chuckled. "Changed your tune? Okay by me. At least I won't have to hold your hand and walk you to the bus when school starts next week; you'll have Shari Ann to protect you."

Josh opened his mouth to say something mean, then realized that Benji just might know he was in trouble with the Titans and that maybe he was trying to distract himself and them from thinking about it by being difficult.

"And how about that Sheridan kid, huh?" Benji crumpled the plastic bottle in his hand. "Tell me that kid is really thirteen, and I got some swampland I wanna sell you. Thirteen? C'mon. More like sixteen. Kid's got a mustache, I swear."

"Coach Swanson's not going to have someone who can't qualify." Jaden patted the folder she kept with the team paperwork in it.

"Yeah? Show me that kid's birth certificate. Let's see it." Benji spun around in the front seat.

Jaden dug into the file she kept for the team. She flipped through all the copies of birth certificates, then went through them again before she looked up. "I can't find it."

"Because it's not there." Benji gave a short nod. "Like I said, that kid is not thirteen. No one on our roster's going anywhere except Coach Swanson when

173

my mom gets done reporting him."

Josh looked at Jaden. "Benji, just 'cause he's big doesn't mean Sheridan is older than us."

Benji just shook his head.

"Report him to who?" Jaden asked.

"That BARF or whatever they call that league we're in."

"Whatever you need me to do, Benji." Benji's mom reached over and patted his knee.

"It's 'Y-bell,'" Jaden said. "'Y-B-E-L.' Where'd you get BARF?"

Benji waved his hand impatiently. "Whatever it is, Barf, Y-bell, High-bell, I don't care. Why are you always getting bogged down in the details?"

"Well, I'm a journalist," Jaden said. "Details are important. And this could be exactly what I've been looking for." Jaden clapped her hands and rubbed them together. "This could be perfect. You win your house, and I win the Young Journalist Award. College scholarship, here I come. If I can prove—with some serious investigative reporting—that Jack Sheridan is fourteen, I can't miss. It's my ticket, guys. It's just perfect."

Benji nodded. "Women are devious. My dad told me."

Jaden frowned. "I think your dad got hit in the head too many times. You can't just say women are devious."

"What about free speech?" Benji asked. "Miss Smarty-Pants *journalist*."

Josh looked at Jaden to see how she'd respond. He'd

174

heard plenty of lectures from her about the freedom of speech.

She twisted up her lips. "Yup. Free to say something, even if it's totally nuts."

Benji fought back a victory smile. "And, while I know I said devious, I also gotta admit, you're smart. Very smart."

"Glad you think I'm smart," Jaden said.

"You know I do. I just have to keep your head from getting overinflated," Benji said. He turned to Josh. "Josh, ask your dad the best way to report a crazy coach with an illegal player to the league, will you?" Benji asked.

"Before or after I tell him how you said he burned us?" Josh couldn't help tossing out the barb.

"Me and your dad are alpha males. We can take criticism from the pack. I don't expect you to understand, buddy, but trust me. Me and your dad?" Benji thumped his chest. "We're tight."

"You shouldn't say 'illegal player,' Benji. You don't know that at all," Jaden said.

Benji held out his hand. "Talk to the hand. My instincts are like a ninja's."

Benji's mom took the corner sharp enough to dump Benji in her lap. She patted his head. "You just tell me who to call."

CHAPTER THIRTY-NINE

"HE *WHAT?*" JOSH'S DAD sounded tired.

Josh knew his father was in Texas, in a roadside motel somewhere between Dallas and Austin, maybe a place called Golinda or Golando. He had already explained the situation with Benji possibly getting cut from the Titans. "Ran him all practice. Benji got sick, and the new kid's crazy good, Dad."

"Yeah, but good doesn't mean he's not thirteen," his father said. "You can't go accusing a coach of something like that. He'd be banned from YBEL for life if he did something like that, not to mention what Nike would do. Swanson's supposed to be an up-and-comer. I doubt it, Josh. And just because he didn't *have* the birth certificate in there with the others doesn't mean he doesn't have it somewhere. You said the kid just moved into town, so . . ."

They were both silent for a moment.

"How's it going, Dad?" Josh hadn't told him about Bricktown, and he didn't want to. There was nothing his dad could do and no sense in making him miserable too. Josh knew his dad didn't like bad news even in the best of times.

"I'm tired, but I met some good prospects. A heck of a pitcher in this town. The parents seem to like me."

"Don't you miss being here?" Josh asked.

"I miss you and your sister." Josh's father's voice changed. "But I'm doing what I love, Josh. Everything comes at a price. That's life."

"I guess." Josh looked around his room. It was late, and he had most of his things in boxes. Only the trophies on his dresser top waited to be packed. He took down one of the big ones and protected it with the bubble wrap his mom must have brought just for that since it was sitting on his dresser.

"Well." His father sighed. "I best be getting some sleep. Early start tomorrow. Headed to Laredo, and I gotta meet a high school coach for breakfast. Looks like a four a.m. departure for me."

"So, what if Mrs. Lido wants to call anyway. Can she?" Josh rolled up some underwear from his drawer and packed it around the big trophy.

"It's a free country," his dad said, "but you better kill the king."

"What's that mean?" Josh let another pair of underwear dangle from his fingers.

"It means, if Mrs. Lido goes after the coach, she better make sure she's gonna get rid of him. If you go after the king and you don't kill him, you're in for a world of hurt."

"I don't think Benji has much to lose."

"Well, I can't believe Swanson's really thinking about letting Benji go," Josh's dad said. "He was one of our better players. He's got the arm for an outfielder and moves better than you'd think. Also, he gets you a home run every so often. But if she really is determined to pressure Swanson, tell Mrs. Lido to give Ty Rylander at Nike a call. Nike has more resources and will get more uptight about this than anyone, and if something is amiss, they can fix it without making a mess you can't fix with the league. Trust me, but *you* stay out of it, all right?"

"I will." Josh wasn't going to tell his dad why. He didn't want to *say* he was going to keep trouble free because he planned on getting to the Home Run Derby and winning his mom that house. He just wanted to *do* it. He recalled his session at the batting cages when he'd been really banging them. He wasn't certain they were real home runs, but they were solid hits for sure. And he knew it was very different when you were hitting against a live pitcher instead of a machine, but he was confident he'd get those twenty homers to qualify and then . . . in Houston? Why couldn't he plunk one into that bathtub?

As soon as Josh hung up the phone, his mom came into his room. Josh wondered if she'd been listening at the door.

"I see you're mostly packed. Good work." His mom took one of the trophies off the shelf and packed it alongside the other one, snugging it up next to the bank of rolled underwear.

"Yeah. Well . . ." Josh took another one down and laid it in.

"Everything's going to work out, Josh." His mom touched his cheek. "We have each other."

Josh wanted to brush her hand away but didn't. "Okay."

"I mean it."

"Fine." He tried to sound pleasant, like he believed it.

When everything was packed, Josh texted Jaden, who had dropped her idea to write about concussions because the idea of exposing age-related cheating in youth baseball was something she said she could sink her teeth into. And, with a possible example of it on the Syracuse Titans, she was certain she could get it published in the *Post-Standard*. Then he texted Benji Ty Rylander's name and said he was at Nike and that his dad said he was the best person to file a complaint with. Benji texted him back, asking if Josh had the guy's number.

Josh sighed, sitting alone on his bed, texting and talking aloud to himself. "Really, Benji? Can't you Google it? It's Nike. Call the main office, right?"

Benji texted back that their internet was down, and his mom wasn't doing searches because she was out of data for the month.

"Fine," Josh said aloud, dialing his father again.

He got no answer and figured his dad had shut off his phone. Josh sent him a text, then texted Benji back that he'd have to wait until the morning when his dad was up. Benji wanted to know why Josh's dad was in bed so early. Josh didn't reply and instead shut off his phone. He climbed into bed and lay awake. Even with his eyes closed, he could see himself taking that perfect swing and connecting, could see the ball clear the fence as he ran down the first-base line, slowing into his home run trot. Home runs. He'd get his first crack at them this weekend. He knew he could get twenty.

He had to.

CHAPTER FORTY

THE NEXT DAY WAS Thursday. Friday they'd travel to their first YBEL tournament at Harvard University in Cambridge. Josh's mom got a couple of guys who'd worked at her old job to help load up a U-Haul truck. Josh pitched in, even though he was dying to get back to the batting cage. He couldn't let his mom do it alone, especially because Laurel was buzzing around like a bee. The whole thing to her was a wonderful game because she was going to get to share a bedroom with her mom.

She had no idea.

"We gonna put pink ribbons on the walls, Joshy! And we gonna hang Baby Bop and Barney from the ceiling so they can watch over us if we get scareded at night."

Josh reached over to tickle her. Laurel squealed and danced around the kitchen table before the two men picked it up, turned it sideways, and carried it out. Much of their furniture was staying. His mom was having a house sale over the weekend before she handed the keys to the bank. Josh was glad he'd miss it.

The day outside was promising sunshine and a blue sky. Inside, Josh was the exact opposite, pure gloom. His mom oversaw the two men loading up the first of the two runs they'd need to get everything while Josh watched Laurel. She wanted to play on the swings in the backyard. Josh got a text from his dad with the number for Ty Rylander. He was just about to forward it to Benji when a shadow fell across his phone. Josh blinked and looked up.

"Coach? What are you doing here?"

Coach Swanson gripped the swing set's frame, leaning against it with one hand. "Hey, LeBlanc. Your mom was on her way out, but she told me you were in the backyard. I came by to talk. That okay?"

Something about the coach's face made Josh close his fingers around the phone. He slipped it into his pocket. "Sure."

Coach Swanson looked up at the sun and smiled at Laurel.

"I can swing high!" she hooted.

"You sure can." Coach Swanson laughed, but it sounded forced to Josh. "This your little sister, Josh?"

"Yeah. She's three."

"And a *half*." Laurel giggled.

"Nice." Coach Swanson's smile dropped from his face as he turned to Josh. "LeBlanc, I need to ask you . . ."

"Sure, Coach." Josh felt his stomach tightening.

"This business about Jack Sheridan."

Josh remembered Benji's big mouth talking about getting Coach fired. He thought about Jack Sheridan being in the dugout with them, maybe listening, and he felt the sudden urge to run.

CHAPTER FORTY-ONE

JOSH COULDN'T RUN. HIS little sister was swinging in the sunshine, and he was supposed to watch her. It was an effort, though, to keep his legs from carrying him away. He'd leap the fence and just keep going down the street without stopping until he reached Jaden's house. She'd know how to handle this situation. Josh sure didn't.

"Uh . . . Sheridan?" he said.

"Yeah." Josh thought he saw a slight pulse in the coach's scalp, just below the scar. "He's gonna help us win this season. I know you want that."

"I do."

Coach Swanson nodded. "I noticed a sofa out by the curb. You getting rid of your sofa?"

"Well." Josh felt relieved to be off the Jack Sheridan subject. "We're moving."

"Ahh. I saw the sign. Thus your eagerness to win that derby, right? It's kind of coming together for me now."

Josh felt as if he were standing there in his underwear, ashamed and helpless.

"I'm watching my sister. My mom will be right back."

"Good. Hey, I was wondering," said the coach, "did you ever meet Ty Rylander when your dad was coaching?"

"Ty Rylander?" Josh stuttered.

Coach Swanson studied Josh. "He's the Nike brand manager for baseball. You know, sometimes people think someone on a Nike team is cheating or something. Maybe using pine tar on the ball, or Vaseline, something like that. The man they call is Ty Rylander. He runs it down. Nike wants everything good . . . for the brand."

Josh tried to look surprised. "They have a guy who just does that?"

"Your dad never told you about him? You guys never had someone complaining when your dad ran the team? Even when you ripped through that national championship?" Coach Swanson looked up at the sun for a moment as if listening. "People are always griping about something or other when you're on top. It's jealousy mostly."

"Well, if they did, I guess my dad didn't say much about it."

"Nice. Well, I wanted to point out to you that if anyone

started making a stink with Ty Rylander, complaining, you know, about . . . I don't know—anything—well, they might just shut the team down. *Bang!*" Coach Swanson snapped his fingers like a firecracker, and Josh jumped. "Just like that, it's over. The whole fall ball, and that'd be a shame for your home run derby plans, right?"

The coach let that sink in before he continued. "Look, I'm telling you Jack is thirteen, Josh. We're not breaking any rules. I need this job just like you need your home run derby. And you're the one who can shut this rumor right down, Josh. Benji will listen to you, and the team will listen to Benji, and we can put this whole ridiculous thing behind us." The coach leaned back. "I'm glad we got to talk like this, Josh. Just you and me."

"And me! I'm talking!" Laurel shrieked from the swing as her shirt flounced up into her face at the high point.

"Yes, you are." Coach Swanson turned and grinned at her. "You're talking good. And you keep swinging!"

"I'm going to the moon!" she howled.

"Me and your brother will have to get a rocket ship and meet you." Coach Swanson patted Josh on the shoulder. "We're a team." He waved to Laurel. "You hang on tight! Good-bye!"

"Bye-bye!"

Josh watched Coach Swanson stalk around the corner of the house without another word. He fumbled with his phone, digging it free from his pocket and dialing Benji.

"Heavy hitter two, at your service," Benji said.

"Benji. Come over here." Josh was breathless. "We gotta talk."

CHAPTER FORTY-TWO

JOSH CALLED JADEN AND got her to come over as well. The three of them sat on the back steps, watching Laurel. Josh knew his mom would be home any minute.

"Dude, what's this all about? What's so top secret that you couldn't text me or tell me on the phone? And why are you here?" Benji gave Jaden an insulted look.

"I'm the brains," Jaden said.

"I wanted an unbiased opinion," Josh said. "Benji, you can't call Ty Rylander."

"What? Your dad didn't have the number?" Benji wore a Titans cap, and he pulled it down low on his brow. "Our internet should be up soon. If not I'll go to the library and Google it. That's not such a big deal."

"No, I mean you can't call him. Not now, not ever. I won't be able to get into the derby if there's a stink."

"Now that's a problem." Benji flipped the brim of his hat up so they could see his face in all its horror, anger, and shock. "Are you telling me you don't *want* me on the Titans? Dude, I know you can't be saying *that*. Who hit the winning home run in the national championship game at Cooperstown? Was that Jaden? Was that Esch or Sheridan or *you*?"

"You hit it, Benji," Josh said.

"Yes, I did." Benji's face showed great satisfaction. "And how about that diving catch I made in Albany in the World Series qualifiers? This Swanson knows none of that, and he's ready to cut me because why? I'm big boned? So I can't run like a deer. Big deal. Remember the Babe? Who doesn't know Babe Ruth was big boned too? Swanson deserves everything he gets, and when my mom unleashes the Death Star, he's gonna wish he never heard of Titans baseball."

"First, you don't know that Swanson is going to cut you from the team. Second, if you call Ty Rylander and Nike pulls their sponsorship, it'll take weeks to get another coach, weeks I need to be adding to my home run total. And if Jack Sheridan really is older than thirteen, then the whole team might even get disqualified. *I'm* the one who needs a house, Benji. You gotta have mercy on me." Josh sniffed and looked away. "I mean, Bricktown?"

"Dude, you cannot be crying," Benji said.

Jaden swatted him. "Be nice, Benji. Ever since you

hit that home run in Cooperstown you've been a little high on your horse."

"Since I never rode a horse in my life, I'm not even gonna dignify that with a response, Miss Smarty-Pants." Benji swatted at her with his hat. "I thought we were all friends here."

"If we're friends, you'd be thinking about a plan to stay on the team *without* causing trouble with Nike." Jaden scolded Benji with her finger. "I've been thinking about this thing for my story. If Coach Swanson *is* cheating, why can't I find out *without* involving Rylander? I mean, I can investigate it myself, and my article doesn't have to appear until November first—*after* the season and Josh's contest."

"Okay, tell me the plan on just how you're going to do all this and still help me from getting cut?" Benji huffed on his fingernails and wiped them on his shirt. "Go ahead, tell the heavy hitter so he can consider his options."

"I don't have one . . . yet." Jaden looked at Josh. "Do you?"

In that moment it hit him. Josh had a monster idea. "I do," he said. "Poker."

CHAPTER FORTY-THREE

BENJI JUMPED TO HIS feet and paced the grass in front of the steps. "We're talking about serious stuff here, and I'm trying to help out by seriously weighing the heavy hitter's options—and you're goofing around? What does poker have to do with any of this?"

"Like, how you bluff, right?" Josh got excited. "The other person can't see your cards, and you can raise the bet to scare them into thinking you've got a killer hand. They fold and you win, even though you had nothing. But you've got something, Benji. Just don't act afraid."

Benji shook his head. "I don't know. I'm not a bluffer. My face turns colors when I lie."

"Didn't you just lie about not having time to fill out your informational sheet?" Jaden asked. "Painting your garage? Give me a break."

"Now it's okay to lie? See? This is why I always say, leave the girls behind. Like my dad says, they're a devious bunch. Devious, sneaky, very hard to predict, and generally up to no good." Benji snorted at his own wisdom.

"I didn't say it was *okay* to lie." It was Jaden's turn to snort. "You're amazing. Truly amazing."

"Thank you. Yes, that is very true." Benji stood and checked himself up and down with appreciation.

"Look, he wants this Titans job bad. My dad said that he heard Coach Swanson's got plans to advance himself, and there is no way he'd blow it with an over-age pitcher," Josh said. "But cutting you after what you did in Cooperstown would raise some eyebrows. You've just got to bluff like you believe he's got to keep you on the team to keep winning."

Josh didn't tell either of his friends about Coach Swanson's visit. He let them think the warning about Nike maybe dropping the team came from his dad. He didn't want them to know the coach had just shown up at his house. He knew Benji would go crazy. The thought of Coach Swanson appearing like that would send him into panic mode. Then he'd have little hope of Benji's mom not filing a complaint about Jack Sheridan. He knew Mrs. Lido was nothing if not overprotective of Benji.

"There's no harm in it for you, Benji," Jaden said. "If he doesn't pick you today, you can proceed to unleash the Death Star. If he says yes, you're on the Titans, Josh gets his new house, and we all live happily ever after."

Benji stared off into the sky with a big grin. It was as if he could read the clouds.

"What?" Josh couldn't keep from asking. "What are you thinking?"

"Me?" Benji looked startled, then almost a little shy. "Oh, well . . . I was thinking that the heavy hitter *likes* happy endings."

CHAPTER FORTY-FOUR

JOSH'S MOM RETURNED. BENJI and Jaden helped load up the U-Haul for the last time. Then they all rode their bikes over to Woodrow Street to help unload it into Josh's new apartment. Josh cringed and looked around. Halfway down the street, he had to admit to himself that it didn't look so bad in the sunshine. Granted, there were some broken windows here and there, and a doorstep was crowded with sketchy-looking young men, but the trees lining the sidewalks dappled the street with light and shadows.

In the tree right in front of their apartment, a family of sparrows flickered noisily, half a dozen young birds complaining to their parents about being hungry, and the parents working double time to find bugs and crumbs to keep them quiet. The sound gave Josh some hope that their stay on the border of Bricktown wouldn't be so bad, especially since those Qwik-E houses went up fast, and he planned on being out by Christmas.

As he struggled up the steps on one end of a mattress with Benji on the other end, Josh made a mental note to begin to look for building lots somewhere in the Grant Middle School district. He thought there were some out on a dead-end street on the other side of Eighth North Street. Such a thing couldn't cost more per month than this apartment, could it? All they'd need was the lot. He'd take care of the rest.

Josh's mom made them all some lemonade when they'd finished. A breeze wafted through the open windows, lifting the stained curtains the previous tenant had left behind. They sat in the cramped living room on the couch as well as on some of the boxes yet to be unpacked. The guys from his mom's company were fresh out of college, and they talked about how they were looking for work at the mall in one of the new restaurants now that the catering company was no more.

When Josh's mom excused herself to put his little sister down for a nap, he couldn't wait for the young men to leave. Finally, they did, and Josh peeked into the bedroom and saw that his mom had fallen asleep along with Laurel. There wasn't much room in the tiny bedroom for anything but the bed and the dresser. What little floor space remained was covered with boxes.

Josh felt a bit guilty but reasoned that there was little more he could do until his mom got up to tell him where things needed to go. Meantime, he could help the cause by getting himself to the batting cage. Jaden joined him, but Benji begged off, saying his older brother was stopping by, and he'd promised to show Benji a glitch that would help him move up a couple levels in Destiny, his current Xbox rage.

Josh struggled with his first bucket of balls. Jaden had removed her iPad from her backpack, and she pretended not to notice. Josh took a break and asked Jaden what she was writing.

"I can't find anything *new* on this sports concussion angle." She looked totally frustrated and ran a hand through her hair, giving it a little tug, then tying it off in a ponytail.

"You're back to concussions now?" Josh asked.

She threw up her hands. "If your dad thinks there's no way Coach Swanson would cheat, where am I going with that? I don't have time to chase a dead end."

"Wish I could help," Josh said, holding up his bat, "but obviously I've got my own issues to straighten out."

He tried half of another bucket before he threw down his bat.

Jaden swept aside a strand of hair that had escaped her ponytail. "You gotta be tired and sore from yesterday."

"I am, but it's my brain that's more tired and sore

than my body." Josh picked up the bat and swung it over his shoulder.

"All this stuff with Sheridan?" Jaden asked.

Josh scowled, remembering the roller coaster he'd been on for the last half a year. His father had insisted he join the Titans when they were coached by Rocky Valentine, a muscle-brain coach who—without any of the parents knowing—had his team using steroids to make the players stronger. When he, Jaden, and Benji had exposed the coach, Jaden made a name for herself with the newspaper, and Josh's father took over the team. Then that went sour after Josh got hit with a beanball that had shattered his cheekbone. He overcame that and helped his team win the national championship tournament, even though the head umpire was being paid off to make it otherwise. That win had solidified his dad's Nike deal, and Josh believed they were all in for smooth sailing.

That hadn't lasted more than a few weeks, though. The good turned to bad when his father got a new car and met Diane. After that his life had gone into a downward spiral. Josh and Benji and their local team had made it to the Little League World Series but lost. When he and Jaden exposed Diane's involvement in a money scam, Josh hoped his parents would be reunited, but the plan had fizzled and they'd gotten a divorce anyway.

Life was up and down, up and down. He felt like a human yo-yo.

"This Jack Sheridan stuff is one of a lot of things. It's like everything in my life is broken, and there's not much chance of fixing it. I thought that when we busted Rocky Valentine for that illegal steroid thing and my dad took over the Titans, life was gonna be like some storybook. Then we win that national championship? You're writing for the paper? Even though I got my face busted up by that pitch, it was something to overcome, like part of a *good* story."

"Maybe the hard times you're going through now are like that," Jaden said. "Aren't hard times part of a storybook?"

"Not like this," Josh said. "Not your parents breaking apart, then your dad moving a thousand miles away so there's, like, no chance they can get back together; and now we lose our home. . . ."

"But you can get a new one." Jaden's voice rose with excitement.

Josh looked at his bat. "Not like this I can't."

"Let's stop," Jaden said. "You're tired is all. Save up your energy for tonight. You can do this, Josh." Her yellow-green eyes burned at him. "You always do. You always come through. You can start hammering some homers this weekend. Get yourself qualified—I know you will—and then you'll head down to Houston and win that thing."

"You make it sound so good, so easy."

"It won't be easy," she said, "but it'll be good. Come on."

They headed home. Josh went past where he needed to turn because he'd forgotten for a brief moment that he wasn't going to the house anymore. He was headed for Bricktown. Jaden parted ways at the end of his street.

"I don't blame you," Josh said. "It can't be safe."

She waved a hand. "I'm headed the other way is all. I'm not afraid. I'll see you in a few. Mrs. Lido's still picking us up, right?"

"Benji texted me that they were. I better remind them of my new address too." Josh took out his phone and texted Benji as he watched Jaden pedal away, then headed for the apartment.

The sun was beginning to drop, and Josh rode into it, blinking and keeping his lids half shut. When a group of older kids outside a store called out, he wasn't sure they meant him, but he pedaled faster. On the sidewalk a huge skull had been spray-painted, and he thought of the Bricktown gang he'd heard rumors about. His heart was still pounding and his eyes were alert when he reached his door. Josh hopped off his bike, panting. He struggled to pull the bike inside the front doorway to keep it from being stolen. He hurried to get into the apartment, opening the door with his key. Inside, he smelled liver and onions cooking on the stove and didn't think things could get much worse.

"Have fun?" His mom looked up from the stove, bubbling with positive energy.

"Didn't hit too well." Josh crossed the tiny living

room and headed for his own bedroom.

"I unpacked some of your things. Laurel got hungry, so I left the rest for you."

"Can I do it after practice?" He entered the room and dug his larger equipment bag out from under some boxes.

"Sure," his mom hollered from the kitchen. "You can have an early bite with us, then I'll make you something more when you get home. Good?"

He walked out into the cramped living room. She stood tall and pretty with a spatula in hand, smiling like they owned the world. He wanted to hug her. He wanted to cry.

"Thanks, Mom."

"We're gonna be okay, Josh. I know we are."

"Yeah," he said. "We will."

CHAPTER FORTY-FIVE

DURING THE CAR RIDE to practice, Benji announced that he wanted Jaden to pitch in to the effort. "You need to ask Swanson where Sheridan's birth certificate is. I figure that'll turn up the heat even more."

"No way, Benji." Jaden shook her head.

"What do you mean 'no way'? You're part of this team, aren't you?"

"You don't need me sticking my nose in," she said. "You've got to tough it out."

Benji pounded a fist into his open hand. "We gotta let Swanson know what's what. *We* are the Titans. He's a newcomer. We need to school him in the way of the Titans."

"Josh, help me here," Jaden said.

Josh spoke quietly, aware that Mrs. Lido was

listening intently. "I think we're gonna be fine, Benji. Let's go have a great practice and make it impossible for him to bounce you."

"Yeah," Benji said, "but you be sure to let him know that if it ends up going some other way . . ."

"Death Star." Jaden angled her head toward the back of Benji's mom. "We know. We know."

"Benji, I am not a Death Star." Mrs. Lido frowned.

"Tell that to the lady at Walmart." Benji looked back at them, glowing with pride. "This lady sasses my mom at the checkout because you're not supposed to open the underwear to try it on; but you know I gotta make sure it's stuff I can wear, and I don't go for anything when the tags creep into your crack, so the lady says, 'Hey, you opened this underwear; that's not allowed.' And my mom says, 'There's no reason to shout; my son won't wear it if the tag crawls down his crack, so we can't just go buying any underwear we see just cuz it looks good in the package.' So the lady starts hollering and— *BOOM*—Death Star. My mom gets that look, and she's got the manager out there, and he crumbles."

"Well," Mrs. Lido said, "I put up with your father's guff for fourteen years, and I certainly am not gonna take it from the Walmart lady when I'm a paying customer."

"Death Star," Benji whispered to them.

When they got to the field, Benji delivered his paperwork to Martin first thing to avoid any more running.

Soon practice began in earnest. Josh whispered to Benji, "You gotta make some good moves, okay?"

Benji pointed to his chest. "When doesn't the heavy hitter shine like a star? The heavy hitter performs best when everything is on the line. I thrive on pressure like it's an ice cream sundae. It's in my DNA."

Josh wasn't sure if it was Benji's situation, or all the stuff with his parents, or sleeping poorly, or moving to Bricktown, but whatever the reason, he was the one who looked bad in practice, not Benji. Benji shone, and Josh thought that if Coach Swanson was going to base his decision on who to cut on that night's practice alone, Josh would make a fine candidate. He barely nicked the ball in batting practice. Sheridan's pitches screamed right past him, and his arms felt like lead in the field too.

So when Coach Swanson called them all in, huffing and gasping for air, with sweat pouring down their faces and hands on their knees, Josh felt a pang in his gut.

"Okay, men," the coach said. "We're one man heavy. I watched you all carefully tonight, and I've made my decision. It's not an easy thing to do, but if we get an injury somewhere down the line, we'll call you back up."

Josh looked at Benji. Benji panted but gave him a confident wink as if he had it in the bag. Josh wasn't so sure. He didn't trust Coach Swanson.

He didn't trust him at all.

CHAPTER FORTY-SIX

SWANSON LOOKED AT BILLY Duncan and lowered his voice. "Sorry, Billy. It was a tough decision."

Duncan bit his lip to keep it from trembling and concentrated on not bursting into tears. The right fielder stood up and hurried away. Everyone, including Coach Swanson, watched Duncan in silence for what seemed like a long time.

"Lido," the coach said, "I'm switching you to right field."

"Right field?" Benji asked, in shock. "I'm being demoted?"

"Your guess is as good as mine," Coach Swanson barked. "All right. Bus leaves here at 1:00 p.m. sharp tomorrow. You miss it, you know what happens. Now bring it in. No guts, no glory."

They did their chant and broke up. Josh didn't linger. He wanted to get away as fast as he could. Benji was in no hurry and decided to chat with Esch about their prospects in the Harvard tournament. Jaden and Josh waited in silence, then rode home that way.

"All's well that ends well, I always say," said Mrs. Lido when she dropped Josh off in front of his new apartment.

"Yeah, that's true," Josh said. "Thanks for the ride."

"We'll pick you up tomorrow about twelve thirty," Mrs. Lido said.

"I really appreciate you giving me rides all over town."

"You're a good boy, Josh," Mrs. Lido said, smiling. "Benji needs all the good influences he can get."

They pulled away with Benji making a face at him, stretching his mouth wide and waggling his tongue. Josh chuckled and stood still for a moment looking up and down the street. Shadows lurked around the edges of the brick apartment houses and in the doorways. Josh scampered up the steps and hurried inside. His mom had about half the boxes unpacked but said she'd leave the rest for the morning if he wanted to watch *Spirited Away* with her. "Laurel's asleep, and I found the DVD when I was unpacking."

"I thought maybe I'd read before bed?" Josh said.

"I know. You read all the time. You're good like that," she said. "But this used to be your favorite, remember?"

205

He nodded. "I love that movie."

"So let's watch, you and me. Like we used to, okay? I'll make popcorn."

She did make popcorn, and the two of them sat on their couch, surrounded by boxes, watching. Josh rested his head on her shoulder, and she put her hand on his head and gave it a pat every so often. Josh sighed and began to doze.

The movie ended, and his mom helped him into his bed. He fell right to sleep, and his final thought was that tomorrow was the beginning of the most important thing he'd ever tried to do.

It was still pitch-dark when Josh woke to the sound of a gunshot.

CHAPTER FORTY-SEVEN

JOSH'S MOM FLIPPED ON the light. Laurel was crying. Josh felt choked by panic.

"Josh!"

"Mom! What was that? It sounded like a gun."

"I think so." She appeared in his doorway hugging Laurel tight, calming her. "Did you lock the door?"

Josh couldn't remember. His mom darted toward the front door, checking to be sure it was locked. Police sirens began to wail in the distance. The idea of the police heading their way gave some comfort. Josh got up and went to the front window, peering around the edge of the curtain. "There're people out there."

"Get away from that window!" His mother's scared voice made Laurel begin to cry anew. "There, there. It's okay. Mommy has you."

Josh backed away. He didn't say anything to his mom. He didn't have to. They knew what they were both thinking. They were only twelve blocks from the place they used to call home, but they might as well have been on another planet.

Josh returned to bed, but his sleep was ruined. His tattered nerves didn't allow anything more than a yawn. When the red and blue lights of the police cars flashed alternately against the living-room curtains and bled through to the corner of his wall across from the open door, Josh sneaked out of bed and peeked around the curtains again. An ambulance had come and gone, and still the police cars lined the street.

When the gray of dawn finally seeped in through the curtains, diffusing the police lights, Josh got up, peeked again, saw nothing new, and sat on the couch to read more of the Tolkien trilogy. It was the only thing that eased his mind in the least, and reading it would pass the time until his mom got up.

She appeared shaken and went right to the curtain. "They're still here."

Josh looked up from his book, reluctant to leave the dangers of Middle Earth for real life.

"Maybe we should put on the news."

"Don't!" His mother had a look as wild as her hair, then her face relaxed. "I'm sorry. Not seeing it won't make it go away, right?"

Josh shut his book. "I'm going to get us out of here.

It'll take the next eight weeks, but I'll do it, Mom."

"Josh, please. Don't put that kind of pressure on yourself. I *will* get another job. I just . . . I need some time, and I can't take just anything. It needs to work with Laurel, right?"

Josh thought of Florida. There he went again, the human yo-yo, up and down. He hated it and knew Florida was a dead end anyway. It would take more than a runaway son or a gunshot to get his parents back together.

Josh stood up and offered his mom a smile. At least they were in it together. "Let me help you get the rest of this unpacked. I bet we can finish before it's time to leave."

"You're a good boy, Josh."

Together they worked. Laurel jangled about between their feet. Josh's mom spoke in the singsong voice Laurel's teacher used in preschool, doing her best to paint a rosy picture and restore some of the magic the two of them had felt last night on the couch. But the magic was gone. Josh ached for the sight of Mrs. Lido's rusty Impala. Finally it came and he was sprung, freed from Bricktown, freed from their tiny apartment and the police tape halfway down the street, blocking the sidewalk and the entrance to another apartment building.

"What happened?" Benji turned around in his seat to stare as they drove past.

"Some trouble," Josh said.

"I bet. Look at that tape!" Benji huffed with the thrill. "The cops are still there. Anybody catch it?"

"I have no idea." Josh looked out the other window, away from the mess.

They got Jaden and made it to the school parking lot twenty minutes early. They were still nearly the last to arrive. Coach Swanson stood outside the bus along with Martin, who had a clipboard and was checking people off.

"Luggage underneath." Coach Swanson nodded his head toward the bus's belly as if this were their first travel game.

They boarded the bus. Josh took a window seat in the back. Jaden took the aisle, and Benji spread out on the two seats across from them, leaning back and sticking two Twizzlers into his nose before chomping on the ends.

"Do you have to be disgusting on top of unhealthy?" Jaden asked.

"Here we go." Benji didn't sound disappointed. "Let the fall ball begin. Here. A peace offering."

Benji removed one of the licorice ropes from his mouth and handed it across the aisle, dangling the chewed and slobbered end for her to take.

"Gross," Jaden said.

"Kidding." Benji pulled a fresh piece from his bag and handed it across. "Peace."

Jaden took it warily. When she realized Benji meant

it, she smiled and took a bite.

Josh opened his book. He wanted to talk to Jaden about the gunshot and the police, but he knew Benji would turn it into a circus. He preferred keeping it bottled up to that.

They got to Cambridge by seven, checked into the Hilton Garden Inn, then had pizza as a team in the dining area. Afterward, Coach gave them an hour to swim before lights-out. During that time he, Martin, and Jaden went over some paperwork at a table set on the tiled floor near the pool. Josh went through the motions, doing cannonballs with Goldfarb, Esch, and Benji, but he was glad when the swim ended. He'd never been so tired in his life.

Josh noticed on the way to his room that Sheridan and Martin were roommates.

"Hope he brought his gas mask," Benji said.

"Come on, Benji," said Josh. "Be nice."

"Well, I can't help it if the kid smells funny."

"Lots of times people can't help it. I think it has something to do with his brace. Maybe he's gotta keep stuff on it to keep it from rubbing his skin."

"Well, I didn't mean anything bad by it." Benji used his key to open their door, sulking a bit and throwing himself down on his bed. "Sorry," he mumbled.

"Who do we play first tomorrow?" Josh asked.

"Ask your girlfriend," Benji said. "They're all the same to me."

"Jaden's not my girlfriend."

"How'd you know I was talking about Jayyy-den? Huh?"

Josh threw a pillow at Benji's head. Benji gave a war cry and jumped across the two beds, catching Josh off guard and body slamming him into the mattress.

"You load!" Josh wrestled out from under him, and they rolled off the bed, each fighting for the upper hand. Josh started to tickle Benji. When Benji started to choke, Josh knew what was next and he bailed out quickly.

"Hey, where you going?" Benji popped up off the floor. "I'm okay. I'm not gonna york."

"I'm going to talk to Coach," Josh said. "See if he's got some tips on any of their pitchers."

"Ah, strategizing. Like Sun Tzu's *The Art of War*. I love that stuff."

"Yeah." Josh closed the door behind him. He didn't want Benji coming along. He really wanted to ask the coach for a favor.

He knocked on Coach Swanson's door.

"Enter!"

Josh saw that the coach had left the chain in the doorframe to keep the door from locking, and he pushed his way in.

Coach Swanson spun around in the chair at his desk. "LeBlanc? What's up?"

"Hey, Coach. Uh, wondering about tomorrow."

"What about it?"

"Just strategy stuff. You know, like *The Art of War.*" Josh forced a laugh because he remembered that Coach Swanson had been in a real war and wasn't sure his choice of words had been the best.

"War is nothing to laugh about." Coach Swanson's voice went cold.

Josh wanted to crawl into a hole. He needed to ask for this favor. It had been haunting him. He had to get out of Bricktown. He had to do every single thing he could to win that house, and twenty home runs wouldn't be easy. The look on his coach's face made him think he should try another time, but he was out of time. They started fall ball tomorrow.

Josh needed the favor now, so he took a deep breath, determined to plow ahead.

CHAPTER FORTY-EIGHT

"SORRY, COACH." JOSH FROWNED and put on his most serious face. "I didn't mean it like that. It's just . . . I told you about that house. I really want to win it, or at least have a chance."

"Twenty home runs is a lot. We only play thirty-two games."

"I know." Josh saw his opening. "That's what I wanted to talk to you about, Coach. See, I'm thinking that if you could move me up in the lineup—maybe the leadoff—that'd be the ideal thing. Then I'd get like twenty to thirty percent more at bats in fall ball. Thirty percent, that'd be huge in helping me—"

Josh fell silent at the sight of Coach Swanson's hand raised in the air, signaling him to stop. The coach gritted his teeth and winced before he spoke. "See, the thing is, LeBlanc, I'm all about *winning,* right? Remember that part?"

"Sure, but I—"

Coach Swanson flashed his hand. "Before you say anything more, tell me this. Why did your dad have you batting fourth?"

"Well, it's cleanup."

"Yeah, what's that mean?"

"I hit a lot of homers." Josh couldn't help feeling proud. "If the first three guys get on and I bang one, it's more scoring. Is that what you mean?"

"Sure. It's baseball 101." Coach Swanson smiled painfully. "Your big hitters bat four and five. Your most consistent hitters are one, two, and three, to get into scoring position for the big bats. For us that's Esch, Goldfarb, and Sheridan. I guess I'm just not sure why it is you're coming to me with something like this. I guess I thought I was pretty clear about why I'm here. To win."

"Yes, Coach." Josh's head dropped. "Sorry. I get it." Even though he was sick to his stomach, Josh really did understand. The game came down to a bunch of little things that all added up. Everything was a calculation of the odds. Swinging at any pitch on a 3–0 count because odds were in your favor. Cheating over just a couple feet toward first against a left-handed batter. Things like that.

"Good," Coach Swanson said. "Get some sleep. You'll

want to be rested so you can get as many home runs as you can . . . batting cleanup."

"Okay, Coach."

Josh returned to his room, watched a movie with Benji, and had another miserable night.

Jaden woke the two of them by rapping frantically on the door like a woodpecker. Benji had set the alarm for 6:30 p.m. instead of 6:30 a.m.

"Nice going, maestro." Jaden sipped her orange juice in the middle of the dining room. "Lucky thing you two have me to help manage things."

"Manage this." Benji thumbed his nose.

Jaden ignored him and peered at Josh. "Not to be a total downer, but you look like somebody ran you through a washing machine without the soap."

"I look better than I feel," Josh said.

"Well, perk up." Jaden tapped her spoon against her glass. "This is the day it begins. You're on a quest. You're like Frodo and Sam Gamgee."

"Hobbits?" Benji raised his eyebrows and stuffed his mouth with sausage. "Josh is a warrior. He's Aragorn, fighting for the survival of his entire race."

"I feel like Gollum." Nothing could bring Josh's spirits up.

He rested his eyes on the bus ride to the fields. The day was gloomy, but the forecast and the tournament officials who checked them in promised the rain would hold off until nighttime, then pass right on through.

When he got off the bus, Martin leaned on his crutch on the curb, holding out his duffel bag. "Coach wants everyone's phones in the bag. No distractions during the game."

Josh turned in his phone, then marched inside with the team. He watched Jaden hand over the folder with everyone's registration form as well as the matching birth certificate, which the tournament official examined before returning to her. When the official got to the last one, he looked around and asked, "Where's the certificate for Jack Sheridan?"

Benji swelled up, looking ready to crow.

Jaden shrugged and shook her head, but before she could say anything Coach Swanson stepped forward and handed the official a large manila envelope. "Jack just moved up from North Carolina, and we had some issues finding the original birth certificate, but I've got it now."

Benji's mouth dropped open, and Josh had to admit he was also surprised.

The official nodded and accepted the envelope. He looked only briefly at the papers inside. "I see. Of course. The Titans are on field three against the Louisville Lions. Good luck."

The team headed out of the field house and down the walkway to field three. Louisville was already there, warming up in their black-and-gold uniforms. The

Titans looked almost harmless in their dark-blue shirts and white pants as they milled into the dugout and deposited their gear. The Lions' pitcher was warming up on the mound. He had a sidearm release and some kind of crazy action on his ball that Josh had never seen before. It looked like the worst kind of pitch to try and knock out of the park.

"What are you thinking?" Jaden caught him staring from the dugout.

"That's just a nasty pitch." He nodded toward the mound.

"You can do it, Josh. You're the best."

"Maybe when the game gets going. I'm a gamer, right?" Josh looked into her green catlike eyes.

"You *are* a gamer, Josh; you're the best young player anyone's seen." She had dropped her voice to nearly a whisper.

Josh felt a charge of adrenaline. It meant a lot for her to say that. In all the tumult, he'd forgotten that at the bottom of all this, he *was* an outstanding player. "Thanks."

"Go get 'em." She gave him a slap on the back, and Josh charged out onto the field.

CHAPTER FORTY-NINE

AFTER WARM-UPS THE TITANS took the field. Out on the diamond at second base, Josh muffed an easy grounder, and the batter reached first on his error. As quick as a blink, the confidence Jaden had inspired flew from his spirit. Sheridan threw a fastball on the first pitch to the next batter that got knocked over the fence. Just like that the Titans were down by two runs. Thankfully, Sheridan struck out his next three batters.

The Titans jogged into the dugout.

"You gotta make that play," Coach Swanson growled under his breath without looking up from his clipboard as Josh passed him. Josh tried to clear his mind. Benji thumped him on the back. "You'll get your mojo. You're a heavy hitter. No worries."

Benji was wrong. Josh didn't even get a chance to hit

in the first inning. Called Stomper by his teammates, the Louisville pitcher sat the first three batters down, including Sheridan, with just fourteen pitches. The game turned into a pitching battle, with Sheridan ending the beginning of the second inning almost as easily as the Lions' pitcher ended the first.

Josh retrieved his bat and batting helmet from the dugout and stepped right up to the plate. The error was still on his mind. His father was on his mind. Bricktown was on his mind and the gunshot too. What wasn't on his mind was hitting, and he felt a sudden and wild fury with himself. He *needed* to hit home runs. Stomper eyed him, grinning like a dog when it finds a half-eaten hamburger. Stomper wound up and delivered his deceptive sidearm pitch. Josh swung for the fence, and missed. Three times he swung, and three times he missed, one right after another.

Josh banged his bat in the dirt.

Coach Swanson stood with his clipboard, straight and strong and frowning. "You're trying to kill it. Let's just get a *hit* next time up."

Josh ground his teeth, knowing the game would keep going downhill for him from there. He had a second gaffe in the field. It was a play he would normally make, a diving grab at a line drive that put a Louisville runner on first. The good thing for the Titans was that Sheridan was red hot. It wouldn't be totally accurate to say that Jack Sheridan won the game single-handedly, but it wouldn't be far from the truth.

Sheridan shut Louisville out after a fourth-inning double, and on offense he had a home run in the fourth to put them within one. After Sheridan's big hit, Josh stepped up and swung for the fences himself, ignoring Coach Swanson's reminder just to get a hit. Josh whiffed the first two pitches and knew he had to swing at whatever came to protect the plate. The ball came in high.

Josh swung.

CHAPTER FIFTY

JOSH DIDN'T WHIFF. HE nicked it and stayed alive. Stomper's grin faltered. He threw another, and Josh got a piece of that one too, fouling it into the backstop. Josh felt like he had a handle on the action of Stomper's sidewinding pitches. Stomper wound up and threw. Josh smashed it, feeling the power of his swing. In that moment it all came together for him. He could feel it. He could see it.

A home run. He'd tie the game. It was the beginning of his quest.

As he tore down the first-base line, he realized the ball had gone higher than he would have liked. The Louisville player in left field was sprinting toward the fence. Josh rounded first. The ball fell fast; the defender stretched his glove.

And caught it.

The sound of his bomb smacking the player's glove hit Josh like a lightning bolt. He staggered to a stop, slouched, and shuffled back to the dugout.

Coach Swanson spoke through his teeth. "I *said* a *hit.*"

Jaden gave him a sympathetic look, but the rest of his teammates didn't even look at him as he sat on the end of the bench.

It wasn't until the end of the fifth inning that Stomper started to fade. He gave up two hits and had runners on second and third before just barely getting out of the inning. The Lions were ahead 3–2 at the top of the sixth, but they didn't get another run off Sheridan. The Louisville coach replaced Stomper in the bottom of the sixth with a kid built like a fireplug who threw nothing but overhand four-seam heat and right down the middle. Josh was licking his lips in anticipation.

The Titans' eight-hole hitter whiffed, but Preston, at the bottom of the order, was hit by a wild pitch.

With one out and a man on first, Esch, the Titans' leadoff hitter, fouled off half a dozen heaters and finally struck out on a fastball he just couldn't catch up to.

Then Goldie smacked a double. Preston, afraid to make the last out at home, stopped at third. Goldie held up at second.

With the winning run on, Sheridan stepped into the box. An outfield hit with two out would win the game since both runners would be moving on contact.

Josh stewed in the dugout, knowing that he could crush a ball off this guy and win the game. It would be a piece of cake to go hard on a pitcher who threw nothing but flat, middle-of-the-plate heat. All the bad stuff could be erased. But Josh rooted hard for Sheridan anyway.

"Come on! You can do it!" he shouted along with the others. Then he remembered the derby. If Sheridan won the game, Josh wouldn't get to hit.

Jack Sheridan did it, all right. He sent a line drive right over the second baseman's head. It skittered between the outfielders and clattered against the fence. The runners on second and third scored. Sheridan took a bow from second base toward the howling Titans dugout. His two-RBI double ended the game.

The only one not cheering was Josh.

CHAPTER FIFTY-ONE

THE TITANS' BUS TOOK them to lunch at Legal Sea Foods in downtown Boston. Several tables had been reserved for the team. Sheridan sat with Coach, Goldie, Preston, and a couple others. Esch sat with Josh and Benji.

Jaden came in talking to Martin. She'd gotten to know him as they talked statistics in the dugout.

"This man knows his baseball." Jaden put a hand on Martin's shoulder, and his face reddened. "Come on, sit."

Martin did, and immediately unfolded his napkin and set it on his lap.

"Martin was telling me incredible things about Mickey Mantle, the best switch-hitter baseball ever saw." Jaden looked around at the rest of them. "Like you, Josh."

225

Josh jiggled the ice in his water glass, took a swig, and crunched a cube. He hadn't gotten over not hitting a homer.

"So, he's a baseball genius because he likes Mickey Mantle, who was a Yankee?" Benji wrinkled his nose. "Doesn't sound very impressive to me."

Jaden leaned over toward Martin. "He's only kidding. He's still bitter about Babe Ruth being sold to the Yankees *a thousand* years ago."

"Actually, I'm a Braves fan." Martin spoke quietly and looked at his bread plate. "My dad knew Chipper Jones. . . ."

"Nice," Jaden said.

Martin was obviously uncomfortable, and when the waitress came, she accidently knocked his crutch over. It clattered to the floor, and Martin turned bright red.

Josh was so down about the game, he could barely feel bad for him. Excitement in the rest of the team was high, though, and everybody around them buzzed. Esch ordered the famous clam chowder, and everybody else followed suit. A few minutes after it arrived, Benji looked at Josh's bowl. He'd taken just one spoonful.

"Dude, are you . . . I mean . . . Let's not waste it, right?"

Josh pushed his bowl over to Benji. "Knock yourself out."

"Come on, Josh. It was one game." Jaden scraped the bottom of her soup bowl for the last creamy bite.

Jaden's words didn't help, and the second game later that day wasn't any better for Josh. They won, and he got four at bats; but he only got on base once and that was because of an error by the right fielder, who muffed a pop fly. The other three times Josh struck out swinging for the fences. Benji was the only heavy hitter to knock one over the fence, and that didn't make things any easier. In all the hundreds of baseball games in his life, Josh had never been so rattled. Coach Swanson looked like he'd been chewing glass when he gazed at Josh in the dugout.

That evening at LongHorn Steakhouse, where the team was having dinner, he called Josh aside and said he was swapping him and Benji in the order. It was the exact opposite of what Josh needed. Every spot he moved down in the lineup meant less opportunities to bat, especially with Benji at cleanup. In that spot he'd be an all-or-nothing hitter if ever there was one.

During dinner, Jaden and Martin chattered back and forth about game stats, but Josh barely ate.

Benji jawed a piece of steak and gulped down some milk, leaving a mustache of white foam on his upper lip before he wiped it with his sleeve and leaned across the booth. "Dude, heavy hitters are interchangeable. That's all it is. You can't get down when heavy hitter two takes a turn at cleanup. Come on. How would you feel if I moped when I was batting fifth?"

"It's different, Benji." Jaden gave Josh a worried look.

"He's all twisted up about this Home Run Derby. He's in a slump. Josh, one hit and you're out of this slump."

"You're telling me?" Josh scowled at the forkful of mashed potatoes he let drop to his plate with a clatter.

"Josh, if you don't eat, you'll never hit. Eat."

Knowing Jaden was right, he shoveled in dinner faster than Benji, but he didn't even taste it.

"Dudes." Benji splayed his fingers and lowered his voice. "If heavy hitter two ends up in the derby and wins the house, heavy hitter two is giving that house to heavy hitter one. We are a team. Don't think I want this for myself, but I could win it. I got one home run already. I could get on a hot streak. You never know."

Josh smiled at his friend. "Thanks, Benji. I appreciate that, but I gotta get back to myself. I gotta get into that derby in Houston. It's like I can see that bathtub sitting out there over the fence. I see it in my sleep. I see it when I close my eyes. It's like my destiny. I just gotta get there."

"So," Jaden said, "you relax tonight, get some sleep, and start fresh tomorrow. We play that team from Portland, and I saw the pitcher they're probably going to start the game with. He throws a four-seam fastball too, no movement, straight down the middle how you like it."

"That kid today threw heat. I choked." Josh picked up his fork and let it drop again.

Jaden reached across the table and squeezed his hand. "But tomorrow you won't. You could get two round-trippers in two games and be right back on track. Tomorrow is gonna be your day. I can feel it."

CHAPTER FIFTY-TWO

THAT NIGHT WAS THE first in several that Josh really slept.

He woke early, feeling good, better than he had for several days. Light seeped in through the curtains. Benji snored softly. Josh slipped out of bed, went to the lobby, and logged on to one of the hotel's free computers. He went right to the Qwik-E-Builders website and found the Home Run Derby page. He didn't have to reread the rules; he knew them. What he wanted to do was just stare at the picture of that big red bathtub. It was an old claw-foot thing, and the picture showed it in all its glory, sitting on a tall platform behind the Houston Astros' center-field fence, tilted at an angle so you could probably see it from home plate.

It reminded Josh of one of those games on the

midway at the fair, the beanbag toss where, if you put one through that silly clown's red mouth, you won a stuffed animal bigger than a small kid. The sight of it gave Josh a chill. He felt like he could blast a hit right in there, but instead of a stuffed animal, he'd win a *house*. He visualized it and tried to imagine the sound of his bat cracking and then the *thunk* of a baseball dropping into the tub with a double bang as it banked off the side, hit the bottom, then rolled around, spinning to a stop.

At the breakfast buffet in the morning, he saw Martin trying to balance his tray and work his crutch.

"Here." Josh didn't even give Martin a choice. He scooped up Martin's tray, then stopped at the sight of his face.

"I'm trying to be nice," Josh said.

Martin forced a smile and looked around nervously. "Thanks. I should do it on my own, though, or Coach will come down on me."

"Jeez, is he that bad?" Josh frowned.

Martin shook his head violently. "No, he's not bad. You don't get it. He's right. I don't *want* people feeling sorry for me."

"Well, I don't feel sorry for you. I'm just trying to help. And you can sit with us, right? Don't tell me you can't. Come on."

Sitting next to Benji, Josh dug into his eggs.

Martin picked up his own fork and began to eat.

Jaden had been waiting for a specialty omelet, and she joined them after a few minutes, obviously pleased to see that Josh had invited Martin. She sat down right next to him and patted his arm. "See? Josh knows talent when he sees it too."

"Talent?" Benji blinked at her before chomping on a piece of bacon.

"My friend here has a great baseball mind, Benji. Remember the movie *Moneyball*? Martin has that kind of insight. My bet is he's a big-league general manager one day."

Martin looked down at his plate and shook his head. "No way."

"Martin, come on. Stop being so modest." Jaden looked at Josh. "We sit in the dugout together, and Martin tells me what's going to happen before it even happens. It's crazy. I love it."

"Well?" Josh waved a fork at Martin. "What do you think about my situation?"

Martin chewed a mouthful before he said, "That depends. Are you going to keep swinging for the fences?"

"Well," Josh said. "I'm not sure how well that worked for me, right? I didn't put one out of the park, and I cost myself a spot in the batting order."

"You'll get it back," Martin said. "Sometimes just relaxing is the key. You're the best player we've got. Coach does that lineup thing to his best player sometimes, to get him motivated."

"Not sure if I'm the best player with Jack on the team now." Josh spread some jelly on his toast and took a bite. He wasn't fishing for compliments; he really respected Sheridan's skill.

"Forget hero worship." Benji leaned into the middle of the table, wanting to be heard. "You gotta just play baseball. Get back on track. Do not get distracted."

Benji pointed his finger at Josh, and even though Josh suspected his words were a string of lines he'd probably stolen from the movies, Benji was right.

Josh just had to play.

CHAPTER FIFTY-THREE

IT WAS THE PERFECT day to get back on track. A front had moved through, leaving a trail of high, wispy clouds, sunshine, and a bite of a breeze hinting at autumn. Hard-core baseball fans and devoted parents from around the country crowded the stands. Crimson Harvard balloons were tethered to some kids' wrists while others escaped to float high and free out over the Charles River, hurrying toward the ocean. Josh inhaled deeply, catching a hint of grilled onions and chicken from a vendor whose truck shouted "Souvlakis!" with its sign and smells.

The Portland pitcher Jaden scouted was the one who did indeed start the game. And as promised, he had a strong arm and a heavy fastball. Most of his strikes came in knee level or lower. He struck out the first two batters before giving up a single to Sheridan. Benji, he hit with a pitch. Benji went down like a side of beef, but recovered and waved before jogging down the first-base line.

On deck, Josh took a final swing and glanced back into the dugout. Jaden sat shoulder to shoulder with Martin, who was bent over some papers. She clenched her fist and raised it, mouthing the words, "You can do this."

He stepped into the box. The first pitch came in fast and low. Josh tried to get under it and missed. The next pitch was way outside, and he let it go. In came a ball above the letters. A small voice inside Josh's head screamed for him to let it pass, but his heart said, "Go get it," and he did, banging it out of the park, but fifty feet foul of the first-base line.

"A hit!" Coach Swanson screamed, his face like a boiled lobster's. "We got two on! LeBlanc! Get me a hit!"

Josh's hands were sweating so badly he thought about pulling off his batting gloves, but he wanted to get on with it. He wanted that next pitch. He wanted his first home run, to break his slump and move on with his quest. He rubbed the rosin glove on his bat handle and tightened his grip when he dug back in.

The pitcher's eyes swam with doubt, maybe even fear. Josh's explosive hit confirmed that whatever the pitcher had heard about the power of his bat wasn't an exaggeration. The pitcher licked his lips and blinked a couple times, then wound up and let one fly. It was knee high, his best pitch. Maybe it would drop out of the strike zone, maybe it wouldn't. Josh wasn't going to wait to find out. He dropped his shoulder just a bit to get his swing up under it. If he could tag this pitch, it would go a mile.

As if time slowed to a crawl, Josh watched the ball come, saw the spin, and swung. The bat clanged like a fire bell, clear and true.

The ball took off for heaven.

CHAPTER FIFTY-FOUR

IT NEVER MADE IT to heaven, or if it did, it got spit back down.

The center fielder backpedaled, got his butt right up to the fence, raised his hands, and hooted as the ball dropped into the pocket of his glove. Josh gripped the bat, and it trembled beneath his fingers. He wanted to throw it into the dirt, into the dugout, into the face of his mean coach. Instead, it shook in the double clutch of his hands, draining the anger and frustration from the rest of his body. Josh clenched his jaw so hard his head hurt.

Even Coach Swanson kept quiet when he saw Josh's face. Josh said nothing, but got his glove and went out to second base. He ranted to himself and fumed, blowing off steam as best he could without simply pulling his hair out of his head and spinning around like a complete nut case. He didn't get another at bat until the end of the third inning. They had a 1–0 lead, thanks to a double by Sheridan and an RBI double by Benji. Josh breathed deeply, not wanting to leave the on-deck circle until he calmed himself.

Jaden came out of the dugout wearing her Titans uniform and carrying her clipboard. She patted his back. "Go do this."

Josh nodded, knowing that he could. He approached the plate.

After two pop-up foul balls and a 0–2 count, Josh struck out swinging at a fastball so low that it actually hit the catcher's foot. He gritted his teeth and stormed back to the bench, avoiding eye contact with everyone.

He got up one last time in the sixth inning, this time facing a less-talented pitcher who laid one in on the first pitch. Josh got under it and blasted the ball for all he was worth. It went so high Josh lost sight of it, then came down without the right fielder having to move more than three feet to get under it. They won the game, but Josh felt worse than he had the day before.

Their final game—the championship—would be played that evening, and as they got on the bus to head back to the hotel, Josh couldn't even speak, not to Benji, not even to Jaden. He hid beneath an angry scowl with his hat brim pulled low and ear buds jammed home with music from his iPod so loud others could hear it.

Not stopping in the lobby, Josh hurried to his room, kept his music on, and buried his nose in *The Return of the King*. Benji knew to leave him be. Jaden tried to get him to text her back, but he ignored her and read, losing himself in the story. He was almost there, caught up in Frodo's scary encounter at the gates of Mordor, when someone started hammering the door without stopping.

Josh yanked the buds from his ears and shouted, "What! Leave me alone, Jaden!"

Silence for a moment before he heard a voice that wasn't Jaden's. "It's me. Josh! Answer!"

It was a voice Josh didn't recognize. He rumpled his brow and got off the bed, approaching the door slowly. He put his eye up to the peephole.

When he realized who it was, he took in a sharp breath.

CHAPTER FIFTY-FIVE

JOSH HAD NO IDEA what Jack Sheridan was doing there. He'd changed out of his uniform and was wearing jeans and a T-shirt. His dark hair was matted and wet, like he'd taken a shower.

He was carrying his bat.

"What do you want?" Josh asked through the door.

Jack rattled the handle and knocked with the bat. "Let me in. I gotta talk to you."

Even as upset as he was, Josh couldn't resist. He opened the door. Sheridan looked up and down the hall as if checking to make sure the coast was clear, then stepped inside, closing the door behind him.

"Why are you here?" Josh kept his eyes on the bat, nervous now for some reason.

Jack walked past him and sat down in the chair by

the curtains. Josh didn't sit down but stood at the foot of his bed.

"Where's the big guy?" Jack looked around and planted the bat on the floor in front of him like he was staking a claim.

"Probably at the pool."

"Probably at the snack bar." Jack smiled.

Josh didn't smile. "Could be. Why are you here?"

"You don't like me, do you?" Jack leaned forward with both hands on the end of the bat.

"I don't even know you."

"True." Jack raised and eyebrow and pointed at Josh with the fat end of the bat. "But you and I got a lot in common."

"We do?"

Jack nodded. "This—the game—is important to us. I mean, it's important to everyone, but you and me? It's something more. It's like life or death."

"Not quite." Josh swallowed.

"I don't believe you. Look at you." Jack jiggled the bat at him. "You're a mess."

"I'm fine. I'm in a slump."

"With time running out, right?" Jack thumped the floor with the bat. "We just played about ten percent of our fall ball season already, and you've got a goose egg in the HR department. Coach told me that you want that house."

"It's none of your business, Sheridan." It felt like the

coach's favorite was in complete control, and Josh didn't like it.

"You're doing it wrong." Jack's dark eyes sparkled. He stood up and reared back with the bat in both hands now, ready to take a swing. "Yeah, I can help you. It's easy."

Josh stuttered. His insides were doing flips and twists.

All he saw was a threat.

CHAPTER FIFTY-SIX

"EASY?" JOSH SAID ANGRILY. "Because that's how you roll, right? Everything's easier if Jack Sheridan's involved."

Sheridan lowered the bat just a bit. "Look . . . I see where you go wrong."

Josh's face softened. "Sorry. I'm going out of my mind. I thought you were going to hit me with that."

Jack looked at the bat in surprise, then laughed at Josh. "Hit you? Bro, do I look like a killer?"

Josh let go a nervous puff of a breath, not quite laughter. "I said I'm going crazy."

"That first night of practice, I couldn't believe your bat. I've seen some serious hitters. *I'm* a serious hitter. But you? Your swing packs a punch like you see in the majors. Your speed . . ." Jack looked at him, almost embarrassed. "Anyway, you've got it all—timing, the eye—you know this. But now, all of a sudden, you're uppercutting. I've been watching you. You're trying to jack every pitch out of the park, but you don't need to *try*."

"What? You're saying I can do better if I don't try?" Josh shook his head.

"Yes," Jack said. "I'm serious. Don't give me that look. Let me show you."

Jack got into a batter's stance and in slow motion mimicked Josh's swing. "Your wrists break just here, perfect. Your bat comes through level as a balance beam. You connect with so much power it drives the ball right out of the park. But what you're doing now is this."

Jack brought the bat back again and bent his rear knee just slightly before lowering his back hip down, then up, down, then up again. "You're dropping your back leg, just a fraction. You're dropping your leg to get that upward motion on your bat so it comes through like this. Not flat. More like the upward line of a see-saw, so everything is off. You're striking out, or if you do hit it, you're connecting with the bottom of the ball and sending it up like a mortar."

Josh thought about what Jack Sheridan was saying, and it didn't take him more than a few seconds to realize he was exactly right. Josh let out a gust of laughter. "This is crazy."

"It's not crazy." Jack handed him the bat. "You gotta just be you. Let it happen, you know?"

Josh took a swing, his old swing, and felt its level trajectory.

"That's it." Jack pointed at the bat. "That's all you gotta do."

Josh took a couple more swings, then looked questioningly at Jack.

"Yup." Jack nodded and smiled. "You got it, bro. I can get with you at the park too. You're golden. Back to the real you."

Josh handed him the bat. "I . . . thanks, Jack."

"Hey, I want to win these things. We don't win, and people stop paying attention. Half the reason we came here is because of you. You draw a crowd, and that crowd just might notice me."

"They will for sure," Josh said, happy that in some way he'd be helping Jack too. "Hey, can I ask you something?"

"Sure." Jack smiled.

"Why did Coach tell you about me and the Home Run Derby?"

Jack shrugged. "Everyone wants to win. The better you do, the better it is for all of us, me and Coach included."

"You guys are pretty close, huh?" Josh asked.

"Coach and my dad served together. Look, I don't

want to talk about it." Jack tightened his grip on the bat and began to smack it into his hand.

"I'll see you on the field," Jack said, leaving.

Josh knew how it felt not to want to talk about things. That was for sure.

CHAPTER FIFTY-SEVEN

JADEN CAME WITH BENJI to get Josh for the game.

"He helped me," Josh said.

"What?" Jaden said.

"Who?" Benji asked.

Josh explained how Jack helped him with his swing. "He's right too."

Benji bit at his thumbnail. "I don't know about that. You hit home runs by *not trying* to hit home runs? Heavy hitters just *do* it. It's natural. I guess I can't get into the technical details of how I do it. It's like a snake slithering through grass or a cheetah chasing down an antelope and tearing it to pieces."

"Or a hippo just flopping into a mud hole." Jaden spoke with such seriousness and looked right at Benji so that he was confused into silence.

Jaden clapped Josh on the back. "So, you ready?"

"I think so." Josh blocked everything else out of his mind. When he boarded the bus, he gave Sheridan a thumbs-up but didn't stop to talk. He couldn't get distracted. He couldn't worry about anything. He had to focus. He sat in the back corner by the window and closed his eyes. Over and over he imagined himself taking the perfect swing. It was his own swing, so it wasn't hard to do; he just wanted to repeat it over and over. Josh wanted to see himself hitting the ball out of the park, his way, in his own mind.

Time worked against him. The harder he pushed, the more it resisted; and instead of carrying him along to victory like a swift canoe down a gurgling brook, it oozed along like mud. With Jack Sheridan playing shortstop and Esch pitching, the Titans took the field first, and Josh considered it a good sign when he snagged a soft line drive near second base to end the inning.

The opposing team, a group from Charleston, South Carolina, had a good pitcher too, and he sat down the first three Titan batters, leaving Benji standing in the on-deck circle with a frown. The top of the second inning dragged on, with Esch battling the first two batters, throwing nearly ten pitches to each before striking them out. The third batter got on base with a ground ball that Sheridan fumbled, and the fourth battled it out with Esch before banging one over the fence. Esch showed no signs of weakness, but after a dozen more pitches, he walked the fifth batter.

Josh caught Esch's eye and saw his teammate bite his lower lip, not a good sign. The man on first tried to steal second after the first pitch. The catcher fired a wayward bullet, but Josh leaped up, grabbed it, and slapped the runner's leg to end the inning. Esch jogged over and gave Josh a hug, just how it was supposed to be.

In the dugout, Martin was grinning. "It's back," he said.

"What?" Josh had no idea what he meant.

"Your mojo."

Jaden, looking up from her stats book, agreed.

Josh pushed "mojo" out of his mind and stepped into the on-deck circle. He worked his swing between pitches, studying the action of the ball and visualizing himself hitting it out of the park. Benji struck out and brushed past Josh with a lower lip the size of a small state. "Guy's got a wicked King Felix changeup. You see that thing? Better than King Felix, I swear."

"It's not that good." Josh adjusted the brim of his helmet and started toward home plate, breathing deeply and letting it out slow.

"You okay?" The catcher was a heavy, freckle-faced kid with a Southern accent, and he was trying to get into Josh's head.

"Real good." Josh looked right at him and smiled. "You?"

That shut the kid up. Josh took a practice swing and stepped into the box. The pitcher wasted no time. He wound up like he was throwing to save his own life. Josh watched it, anticipating a hot pitch. It slowed. Josh swung.

"Strike one!" barked the ump.

The catcher snickered.

Josh kept breathing. He knew the kid was going to throw heat, and when he did, Josh was going to kill it, not hit under it but *kill* it.

The pitcher wound up and threw another changeup. Josh whiffed.

He knew the kid couldn't throw three changeups in a row. That would be crazy. Josh gritted his teeth and forced himself to think about the swing. That was all, a nice level swing.

In came the pitch, fast, high, and on the outer half of the plate.

Josh swung and blasted it over the opposite field fence.

He tried not to laugh out loud, but happiness filled him like helium in a birthday balloon. His feet barely touched the bags as he rounded the bases, and a chuckle sprang loose at the way the catcher tried to look like he didn't care. Josh slapped Sheridan, Esch, Preston, and his other teammates high fives. He was so happy.

He had it back: his swing, his rhythm, and his confidence. He was going to get into that Qwik-E-Builders derby.

He just knew it.

CHAPTER FIFTY-EIGHT

JOSH DIALED UP HIS dad on the bus ride home. He got nothing but voice mail, and then a few minutes later a simple text from his dad promising a call later on when he got free. Josh could only imagine that he was on the road somewhere, entertaining players and parents. He wondered where. Some small Texas town, he imagined.

Josh nodded off, and before he knew it they were back in Syracuse. Mrs. Lido was there at the parking lot, waiting for Benji and Josh and Jaden. There were groggy good-byes and congratulations all around. Josh shuddered when he got out of the car on the dark, dreary street and Mrs. Lido pulled away. He scampered up the steps and let himself in. The light in the entryway was out, and Josh's heart galloped until he was safely inside their apartment. His mom was asleep on the couch with a book in her lap, head tilted back and mouth wide open, snoring lightly.

Josh tiptoed around her and got ready for bed. He had just laid down when his phone buzzed.

"Dad?"

"Hey, buddy." His father sounded exhausted. "Sorry, it's an hour earlier here, and I had a dinner."

"How's that going?"

His father exhaled. "Not easy."

"You'll do it."

"I hope so," his father said. "I've never had so many nachos in my life, and I never thought I'd know so much about structural engineering."

"Engineering?" Josh said.

"The grandstands," his father said. "They had to tear them down and start over. Set us back three months at least. Man . . ."

"Well, I've got some good news." Josh tried not to sound too excited, because his father was talking about really big things, a Division One baseball program. "I got my mojo back."

"Your . . . Hey, that's great. Tell me about it."

Josh recounted his struggles and then his breakthrough earlier in the day.

"That's really good. Yeah, relaxing is the key, but I want you to get with that training bat every day. Now that you've got that rhythm back I don't want you to lose it, see? Lock that groove in your mind and keep your bat speed up. Can you do that?"

"Sure." Josh felt a surge of excitement and also a pang of regret. He loved being coached by his dad. He trusted him completely. He also missed him terribly.

"Good. Well, I hate to say good-bye, but I'm ready to fall asleep on my feet." His father yawned into the phone.

"Dad?" Josh felt his eyes welling with tears, and he tried to keep the emotion out of his voice.

"Yeah?"

"I miss you."

His father said nothing for a moment, then cleared his throat. "I miss you too, buddy. More than you can know."

Josh said good-bye. He felt warm all over. Life seemed suddenly good, not perfect but good, and he dropped off to sleep.

The next day Josh got his Speed Hitter going before breakfast. He went right out on the sidewalk, surprised at how quiet the neighborhood was. It was a warm, lazy summer morning, and the only sound was the *thwack* of Josh's practice swing. He actually had a sweat going by the time his mom came out on the steps.

"What are you doing?" she asked.

He smiled and shrugged. "Just getting some hits in." They hugged, and went inside where she fixed him breakfast while he told her about everything that had happened. She set two fried eggs and some whole wheat toast in front of him, and she seemed to glow. "I'm glad you're happy, Josh."

"I'm going to win us that house, Mom." He picked up his fork and dug into his eggs.

She sighed and poured herself a cup of coffee before sitting down across from him. "If you do, I sure won't complain."

Josh grinned at her, happy she wasn't knocking the whole idea. That seemed like a sign to Josh, his mom going along with the whole thing.

It made him feel like it was a mission he was destined to accomplish.

CHAPTER FIFTY-NINE

SCHOOL HAD BEGUN THE day after Labor Day and with it came a flurry of homework, quizzes, and tests. Summer fizzled. The September weeks went by fast, with school and practice and traveling to tournaments every weekend.

Josh got back into his cleanup batting position. His home run count grew and grew, as did his worry over walking down Woodrow Street day after day. If he saw the Skulls gang in anyone's doorway, he'd cross over to the other side of the street and ignore their shouting as he hurried his pace. His mother had a couple near misses with a job. Nothing worked out, and sometimes they ate cereal for dinner while she wrung her hands, fretting.

Josh tried not to be mad at his father, and it wasn't too hard because they didn't get a chance to talk all that much. Between training his college players and recruiting on the road, it seemed they shared more voice messages and texts than they did real conversations. So when they did connect, Josh let the excitement and the love he felt for his dad—despite the bad money situation—win out.

The nights grew cooler and longer, and by late September the Titans were practicing at the Mount Olympus indoor sports facility. Rain turned chilly. Josh and Jack were getting more and more attention. The two of them drew stares and whispers as the word spread about the seemingly unbeatable Titans U13 team.

They got closer too. They talked about upcoming opponents and shared ideas on the pitchers they faced. With Jaden and Martin adding their knowledge, the whole thing felt like the big-time. Josh felt for certain they had a mini-version of the way things went in the majors, where strategy was as important as skill.

His father's life on the road recruiting, the construction delays, and weekend practice sessions with some fairly lame talent at Crosby seemed to be wearing him down. He sounded older and more tired than Josh ever remembered him being, but he loved to hear how well Josh was hitting and kept proud track of the home run count. By late October Josh had seventeen homers in his column and had also secured the promise that if he made it to the derby, his dad would get to Houston to do some recruiting and come watch him for sure.

Jaden got a story into the *Post-Standard* when the Titans won the renowned Atlanta Young Sluggers tournament. She was excited that Josh got two home runs, bringing him to a total of nineteen, but she didn't seem to care much about getting her story into print.

"That's not winning me any scholarship," she said. "But I've got something that might. . . ."

Josh already knew by her behavior that she had something big in the works, bigger than a tournament recap. Sometimes she disappeared for whole afternoons, evenings, or weekend days without any more explanation than that she was working on her Young Journalist project.

Curiosity was eating away at Josh.

"It's better if I don't reveal my sources, but don't worry," she'd say. "I'm not making any waves. I'm being careful. That's why it's taking so long. It'll be great, though, if I get what I need. You're getting the hits to win your house, and I'm getting the facts to win my scholarship."

When Jaden appeared on the school bus Wednesday morning before the big tournament, she had a smug smile on her face and said, "Well, I just got the most important interview lined up. It's exactly what I *need*. That ten grand for college is gonna be awfully nice."

"Chump change," thought Josh. But he liked Jaden so much, he would never challenge her about *needing* the money for college.

He insisted she tell him what the piece was about.

"It's huge, but if I tell you, you have to swear on your life you won't say anything to anyone, especially Benji. I want it to be a surprise, and I want to make sure I can get it all before my sources dry up."

Josh held up an open hand, palm out. "Swear."

"It took me all this time because he's so secretive." Jaden's eyes glowed with excitement.

"Who?" Josh asked.

Jaden narrowed her eyes and lowered her voice. "Coach Swanson."

"What?" Josh was shocked.

"When the Titans go to Pittsburgh this weekend, I'm staying here to wrap this up, and he won't be able to keep it hidden anymore."

"Keep *what* hidden?" Josh asked.

CHAPTER SIXTY

JADEN HELD UP HER phone and showed him the recording mode. "I'm going to interview Jack and Martin's mom and get her on the record. Part of the contest is that you have to have all your sources on audio so they can verify it. They don't want anyone making something crazy up and stealing the show."

"You gotta just stop and tell me what it is," Josh said. "What are you talking about?"

She nodded and looked around to make sure no one could hear before leaning close to him and whispering, "Coach Swanson? The reason he's here? The reason he's got Martin under his wing, and he's grooming Jack to be a big-time baseball player? It's a *blood* debt."

"*What?*" Josh wiggled his ear because he thought he must have heard her wrong.

"I think Coach Swanson is paying back a life. There's this village in Afghanistan in Helmand Province. I'm using pictures of the terrain from the internet so I can describe it: the rock outcrops and caves, everything." Jaden looked around and lowered her voice. "Coach Swanson was out on a mission with a fellow officer to get intelligence from some of 'the friendlies,' but it was a trap. Six Taliban rushed in shooting, and the officer was badly wounded. Coach pulled him to cover and killed four Taliban before the others scattered. Coach Swanson hid them both until a marine evac helicopter arrived. By then his friend was dead."

Jaden looked around again and lowered her voice even more. "They called Coach a *hero*."

"If Coach was a hero, then why is this such a secret?" Josh kept his voice down too, even though it didn't make sense.

Jaden shrugged. "I have no idea, but in every article or news clip I could find about him, it's never covered. One clip I found was from a local news channel in Charlotte—where they tried to ask Coach Swanson about being a hero. He practically beat up the reporter. He wouldn't say anything about it."

"But then how do you know?" Josh thought of how hard-nosed Coach Swanson was, and it didn't surprise him that he'd almost knocked over a reporter. "Did Coach tell you?" It seemed hard to believe.

"No, Martin did. We got to talking about his dad,

and it all came out. Then he got all panicky and made me promise to never tell that he'd told me the story."

Josh tried to keep up. "So the dead man was Jack and Martin's father?"

"Yes! Think about this." Jaden's voice jumped with excitement. "I get Mrs. Sheridan to tell me what happened, and if it's what I *think* happened, hello, scholarship!"

Josh's mind was spinning, not quite understanding what Jaden was talking about, and he asked, "What do you think happened?"

CHAPTER SIXTY-ONE

"I'M BETTING THAT ALL the secrecy around Jack and Martin has nothing to do with Jack being older than thirteen. I don't think that's an issue at all. I think Mr. Sheridan saved Coach's life. I'm betting that he does everything he does for Jack and Martin because he's paying back their dad. How good of a story is *that*? People are already talking about Jack. Now you tie in this war hero thing, a story no one has ever been able to get to? After Mrs. Sheridan tells me, I'll have a source I can bank on without getting Martin into hot water, then I can go to Coach and get the last details. It's my home run." Jaden sat back, grinning.

"But . . . Coach probably doesn't want you to write it," Josh said. "Maybe he's just really private and doesn't want to talk about the war."

"But it's a *good* thing. He's just being modest," Jaden said.

"Does the mom know what you're doing?" Josh asked.

"Well, I told her I write for the sports page sometimes and that I wanted to do something on Jack without him really knowing, and I needed some information about their family background, which is all true," Jaden said. "I . . . I couldn't come right out and say it was about Coach Swanson, because I figured she might not even want to meet. But if I can get her when he's not around, she just might tell me."

Josh shook his head. "I don't know. I mean . . . it seems sneaky."

Jaden punched his shoulder. "Are you trying to make me feel guilty? Look, I put a ton of time into this story. I'm counting on it, Josh. I could win this thing. And it'd be nice to get your support."

Jaden folded her arms, threw herself back in the seat, and looked out the window. Josh didn't know what to say. He'd never seen her so mad. They rode in silence until the bus pulled up in front of the school. Josh tried to talk to Jaden when they got off, but she marched right past him.

"I can't help it if you feel guilty!" Josh shouted after her, but she disappeared into the front of the school without looking back.

Josh felt a thump on his back and turned to see Benji looking sadly at the stream of kids entering the school.

"Can't live with them. Can't live without them."

"What are you talking about, Benji?" Josh asked.

"Women." Benji shook his head, put an arm around Josh, and steered him up the steps toward the entrance. "What's she feel guilty about?"

Now it was Josh's turn to feel guilty. "Nothing."

"Dude, we are a brotherhood. Feminine oaths of honor mean nothing to us."

Josh shook his head. "Nothing. Forget it. Please."

"You can run, but you can't hide," Benji said. "A famous guy—you might know him from the hundred-dollar bill—said, 'Three can keep a secret if two are dead.' You, my friend, are very much alive and have an appointment with destiny in Pittsburgh, so out with it."

"I can't, Benji. Stop it." Josh broke free from Benji's arm and hurried away.

Benji sulked through the rest of the day, and Josh felt suddenly alone. At practice that evening Jaden didn't talk to him, either. He eyed Martin and Jack Sheridan and envied them being brothers. A brother could never walk away. He wondered about their father, though, and if Jaden was really right.

The best thing for him was to forget about it all anyway. He had to stay on point with his own mission. He still needed another home run to qualify. He didn't think that would be hard, not the way he'd been hitting, and from what he'd read online about the teams they'd be facing in Pittsburgh, the pitching was good, but nothing incredible or out of the ordinary. Still, the idea of needing that one more homer gave him the jitters.

At home that Thursday night, after texting with his dad, playing Candyland with Laurel and his mom, and finishing his homework, Josh lay awake in bed. After a soft knock, his mom opened the door and slipped inside. "Hey, honey. What's the matter? You've been kinda quiet tonight."

She put a hand on Josh's forehead, and he let it stay there. Something about the dark and the quiet made it okay.

"I'm thinking."

His mom's hand paused for a moment. "This hasn't been easy, has it?"

"No."

"Want to tell me?" she asked.

"You don't want to hear it."

"Yes, I do. I want to help. Whatever it is, Josh."

He took a deep breath and let it out. "I want to win that home, Mom. There are a couple of lots off Eighth North Street for sale for like twelve thousand dollars. Jaden says with a house on it you could get a mortgage. We'd probably pay about what we pay for this crummy place, only we'd be in a *house*."

It was her turn to sigh. "Well, I can't say I blame you for dreaming, and I'm proud of you for trying."

"I want you to say you're happy that I'm trying."

"It's not your job to win us a house, Josh. These things are one in a million."

"Not that much," he said.

"They're not easy."

"Nothing worth having is easy. Don't you always say that?"

"I don't want to argue," she said.

"Then just root for me, Mom. I need all the help I can get."

"Well, I know you're going to hit at least one home run this weekend. That even I'd bet money on."

Josh grinned up at her.

"I see that smile, even in the dark." She stroked his hair. "You're a good boy, Josh. I love you lots."

"I love you too, Mom," he said. "That's why I gotta do this thing."

CHAPTER SIXTY-TWO

WHEN JADEN GOT ON the bus the next day, she sat down next to Josh.

"Hey," he said.

"Hey."

"We good?" he asked.

"I don't know. Are we?" Jaden looked at him with fire in her eyes and just a touch of sadness.

Josh gave her shoulder a squeeze. "Always."

She gave him a faulty smile. "I'm nervous."

"Me too," Josh said. "It's showtime for both of us. I gotta get a home run this weekend to qualify for that derby. I can't even think about *not* getting it. You, on the other hand, seem to have everything pretty much locked down."

"That's only *if* I can get their mom to talk," Jaden

said. "She might clam up totally when I start asking questions. I have no idea."

"Then what will you do?" Josh asked.

She shrugged. "Maybe next year, right?"

"I know you put a lot into this."

"You can't even imagine," she said.

Josh was happy to have things back to normal with Jaden. She gave him a hug before she got off at her bus stop. "Good luck. I'll be thinking of you. Text me when you get number twenty."

"You got it," he said. "And you text me when you get what you need from your interview."

Jaden looked at the time on her phone. "You guys leave in an hour, right?"

"Yeah, we're meeting at Mount Olympus."

"Well, I'm on my way over to the Sheridans' in about a half hour. There's a bus that changes downtown."

"Let's go, young lady," the bus driver bellowed back at them in the big rearview mirror.

"Go get 'em, killer," Josh said.

They bumped fists, and Josh watched Jaden get off and head up the sidewalk toward her house.

When he got home, Josh threw some last-minute things into his bag. He kissed his mom and sister and hustled outside when he heard Mrs. Lido's horn from the street. Benji was in high spirits because his dad—a huge Pittsburgh Steelers fan—was driving down the next day to watch Benji play in the tournament, then see the Steelers on Sunday night. After the tournament, Benji would stay with his dad, and they'd go to the NFL game together.

Josh couldn't help feeling a little jealous, but he was happy for Benji and also for the bubbly attitude that would make the long bus ride to Pittsburgh more entertaining.

When they got onto the bus at Mount Olympus, Josh couldn't help looking at Martin and Jack Sheridan sitting together across the aisle from where Coach Swanson sat. He looked back and forth between them, thinking of the relationship they all had with each other and imagining there was a pretty incredible story to tell.

"You got a question, LeBlanc?" Coach Swanson startled Josh with his gruff voice and scowl.

"All set, Coach," Josh said. "Ready to knock a few over the fence."

"Let's get a big win in the process, right?" Coach Swanson grinned. "We win this, and it's a clean sweep for fall ball. Think about that going into the spring. The Nike rep told me they're making up special sweat suits for the team if we win this weekend."

"Right, Coach. Four more wins would be big." Josh felt Benji nudging him from behind, and he made his way to the back of the bus.

They played cards for a bit, with Benji shouting "War!" and laughing his head off to the annoyance of those around them. Josh laughed with him awhile but begged off to read. With all the reading assignments they had for school, he still hadn't finished *The Return of the King*, the last of the Lord of the Rings books Jaden had given him. Benji complained but took out his phone and started playing Candy Crush. Josh settled in, using his sweatshirt as a pillow against the window.

He hadn't gotten very far at all before his phone buzzed. He checked the text. It was Jaden saying that she'd got everything she needed from Jack's mom. Jaden had a recording of her telling the whole story about Coach's heroism in Afghanistan and how he'd taken care of the three of them ever since. Josh congratulated her, and she sent a reply.

This story is gonna b HUGE!
I got my home run
now u go get urs!!!
☺

Josh grinned and stuffed the phone back into his pocket.

"What's so funny?" Benji had been watching him.

"Nothing. Good stuff for Jaden. Good stuff for you. Now, hopefully, good stuff for me."

"Heavy hitters." Benji held up a fist.

Josh bumped him and tried to read, but the image of the twentieth home run kept crowding his mind. Josh's stomach fluttered with excitement, but he finally got back into his book.

They checked into the hotel and had dinner next door at Chili's. It was ten o'clock by the time they got back to their rooms. Josh had just closed his eyes when someone pounded on the door three times.

Benji jumped up out of bed and whispered in terror. "Dude, what the heck is that?"

Whoever it was, they pounded again and rattled the door knob.

"LeBlanc!" The voice could only belong to one person. "Open this door before I break it down!"

Trembling, Josh undid the chain and opened the door. Coach Swanson burst into the room and grabbed Josh by the arm.

"You!" Coach Swanson pointed at Benji. "Get to bed. And you!" He yanked Josh out into the hallway and slammed the door shut behind them. "You come with me."

CHAPTER SIXTY-THREE

PANIC EXPLODED IN JOSH'S brain.

Coach Swanson dragged him down the hall. Esch opened the door to his room, peeked out, and closed it quickly at the sight of them. Josh looked back. No sign of Benji.

For some reason, Josh could only think of his father. If his father were close by . . . but he couldn't even call his father. Josh's phone was on the night table. Josh thought about Coach Moose. He might help. Coach Moose might call his father.

Before Josh could even cry out, he was inside Coach Swanson's suite with the door shut behind them.

"Sit." Coach Swanson pointed to an armchair in the corner of the living room beneath a reading lamp.

Josh thought about shouting for help, but he was too

scared. He sat down. Wind blew against the window, and the glass shook. Martin was sitting at the desk with a laptop computer casting an eerie blue glow across his face. He gave Josh a hate-filled look.

"What do you want?" Josh looked at the coach, and his voice broke.

"What are *you* doing?" Coach Swanson said. "You don't talk. Just listen. You get Jaden Neidermeyer down here *with* her phone. I don't care how she does it: her family, your family. I want that phone and the pass code, and you tell her if she shares that audio file with a single soul, your game is over. You want to play tomorrow? You want that home run? That house? You get her down here, and you keep this whole thing quiet."

Josh opened his mouth, but nothing came out.

Martin said, "I told Jaden about the coach, and I told her it was private, but then she goes and talks to my mom and tricked her, and she recorded it!"

Josh could hardly take it all in. They were mad about Jaden's article that would show Coach Swanson was a hero? And why did they want her phone? How could they know if she sent that audio file to anyone? It made no sense. Josh's head was spinning. "Coach, it's a good article. You were a hero."

Coach Swanson trembled, and his face reddened even more. "No. I know what Jaden was looking for—to see if Jack was older than thirteen. And I told you he isn't. And now she's digging into my private life. It's none of anyone's business what happened in the war. You have no idea, LeBlanc. You have no right. . . ."

Josh opened his mouth to explain that it was Jaden's story, not his, but he realized how it looked.

"You are hereby suspended from play for conduct detrimental to the team. I don't need to say anything more than that." Coach Swanson's lip curled back from his teeth.

Looking at his eyes, Josh felt desperate. "Coach, I don't know if I can get her. I can't *make* her do anything. I have to get that homer, Coach. I *have* to."

"Well, that'll be your problem then, LeBlanc. She's your friend, and you're the only one who can stop her. Now get out of here before I do something both of us would regret." Coach Swanson pointed toward the door.

Josh stood up and took a tentative step.

"And LeBlanc," Coach Swanson said, "in case you haven't figured it out, we'll be watching you, so don't even try to get cute."

Josh looked back at Martin, still hunched over his computer, typing away.

Forcing himself not to run, Josh escaped.

CHAPTER SIXTY-FOUR

JOSH COULDN'T ACT; HE couldn't even think. He staggered back down the hall and knocked softly on the door.

Benji opened it. Without a word, Josh entered, shut off the light, and lay down in the dark. Benji's bed creaked as he lay down too. The wind rattling their window filled the silence. Josh's mind was in high gear.

Finally, Benji whispered. "Dude, what the heck? What happened?"

Benji's voice jolted Josh back to reality, and he choked back a sob.

"You okay?" Benji asked.

Josh sniffed, fumbled for a Kleenex in the dark, and blew his nose. "I'm okay. I gotta call Jaden. Benji, you gotta keep quiet about all this. It's serious."

Josh turned on the light, grabbed his phone, and began to dial.

"I don't even know what 'this' is," Benji complained.

"Just . . ." Josh tried to keep from getting angry with his friend, but that's how he felt. "Just stop asking. I can't . . ."

Jaden answered on the third ring in a sleepy voice. "Josh? What's up?"

Josh took a deep breath and told her everything. Benji's face lengthened in horror as the story went on until he put his face into one hand and rested his elbow on a knee. Josh heard him mumbling, "Dude, this is so not good."

When Josh finished, he repeated Coach's ultimatum. He wanted to see Jaden in person, and he wanted the phone.

"My proof."

"Yeah," Josh said. "That."

"Can't I send it?" Jaden sounded scared and nervous.

"You can't like, FedEx it," Josh said. "It's too late."

They sat there breathing on each end of the line.

CHAPTER SIXTY-FIVE

"WAIT," JADEN SAID. "THEY want my *phone*? How do they even know about all this?"

"He said they were watching me." Josh hadn't stopped to think about this, but now that he did it terrified him.

"Your phone." Jaden sounded grim. "You know how Martin collects them before practice?"

"It's like the Gestapo." Benji's voice was low and filled with horror. "The Nazi's secret police."

"Martin was in Coach's room on a computer." Josh said, remembering the blue glow on Martin's face. "His mom told him about your interview. That's how they know. Coach said it was private, that it was none of anyone's business what happened in the war. He won't let me play until he gets that phone."

Silence settled over the three of them.

Jaden finally spoke, her voice heavy and sad. "So I'll come down there. I just don't know how."

"Jaden," Josh said, "I don't know, now that I think about it. I can't really ask you to do this. We're talking about the *chance* of me winning a house. You'll lock that scholarship up for sure with your story. I haven't seen you this excited ever."

"No, I can't do it! I feel terrible. I was kidding myself into believing that Coach would be happy with the story—and worse, I told myself that I wasn't betraying Martin because I'd be getting the story from his mother," Jaden said.

"But what about the scholarship you wanted so much? If anyone deserves that award it's you," Josh said.

"I'll think of something," Jaden said, her voice trying to be strong. "I just don't know how I can get there. I know you're going to win that house. You just need one more homer. I can feel it. It's your destiny, Josh."

"What about your destiny?" Josh felt horrible.

"I need to apologize to Martin," Jaden said, "and to Coach too. I should have known better. I feel so twisted."

"Hey, come on," Josh said with feeling. "I know I like to kid you, but that's one thing you're not."

"My dad's got rounds this weekend," Jaden said. "I guess I could take a bus, but I don't think he'll let me. Staying home alone is one thing, but a bus to Pittsburgh by myself . . ."

"Benji," Josh said.

"What's up?" Benji lifted his head at the sound of his name.

"Your dad."

"Yeah?"

"Did he leave tonight, or is he coming in the morning?" Josh asked.

"Well, you know he had a football game against the Plattsburgh Pirates. I got a text from him. They stomped on their guts, won 70–0." Benji beamed with pride. "My dad had *seven* pancake blocks."

"That's great, but did he leave already?" Josh tried not to be too impatient.

Benji shrugged. "I think he was gonna celebrate a little at the Retreat and come in the morning."

"Can you call him?"

"Now?" Benji looked at the clock. "He's probably wearing a pair of underwear on his head at this point, but I guess I could."

"And ask him if he'll bring Jaden with him?" Into the phone Josh said, "Will your dad let you?"

"If I'm riding with Benji's dad he will. Sure," she said.

"Benji, please. Call him." Josh put Jaden on speaker phone so she could hear.

Benji made a doubtful face, but dialed his dad and put his phone on speaker as well. When his father answered, the background was filled with noise that sounded like an ocean storm.

"Benji boy!"

"Pops, can you hear me?" Benji asked.

"Benji! Get my text? We pounded 'em! We're callin' 'em the Plattsburgh Platypuses cuz they laid an *egg!*"

Laughter roared all around Benji's dad.

"Seven pancakes, Benji boy! Seven! They're callin' me IHOP. Get it? The pancake place? Ha ha ha ha!" Benji's dad erupted with a belch. "S'cuse me, Benji boy!"

Benji leaned into the phone. "Pops, can you bring Jaden with you tomorrow?"

"Tomorrow? What's tomorrow?"

"You're coming to Pittsburgh!" Benji shouted clearly into the phone.

"Plattsburgh? I ain't goin' to Plattsburgh, Benji boy. They'll run me out on a rail after what I did to their defensive line. Ha ha ha ha ha!" More laughter exploded in the background.

"Dad, you're coming to *Pitts*burgh." Benji raised his voice to its limits without it being a full shout. "You are watching me play baseball, then we are going to a *Steelers* game. A Steelers game, Dad. Remember?"

"Steelers! Big Ben, takin' on the dirty Ravens, our archrivals. Yes. We are gonna do that, Benji boy, together!"

"Dad, you gotta bring Jaden with you. *Jaden.* She needs a ride. You have to pick her up."

"Whatever you need, Benji boy, but ya better text your old pa. The concussions are piling up, boy! Text me and don't celebrate too late. You gotta game tomorrow, an' I want you to do me proud. Now, I gotta go cuz it's my turn." The phone went immediately dead, and Josh couldn't help wondering what Mr. Lido had to take a turn at.

"Will he do it?" Josh asked.

Benji shrugged, texting as he spoke. "Got a fifty-fifty chance."

"Fifty-fifty?" Josh tried not to sound outraged. Benji was doing more than Josh could do himself. His dad was a million miles away, and he knew his mom wouldn't dare to try and drive her piece of junk car all the way to Pittsburgh.

"Sorry he was so giddy." Benji plugged his phone into its charger and set it down on the night table. "He gets pretty happy when they win like that, a shutout and all."

"I don't blame him." Josh tried to sound like he meant it. "Maybe you can call him in the morning?"

Jaden's voice squawked from Josh's phone. "Or I can call him? Should I, Benji?"

"Yeah," Benji said. "Sure. Try around seven or eight."

"Seven or eight?" Josh's stomach sank. "Our first game is at nine thirty. He'll have to leave before seven or eight to make it."

"Well, he wasn't gonna make the first game unless they lost and he didn't have to celebrate with his team," Benji said. "He's a professional athlete, dude. You get that, right?"

Josh wanted to explode, but he took deep breaths in through his nose and tried to let them out slow.

"You okay?" Benji asked.

"Josh?" Jaden said from the speaker phone.

Josh was determined not to say anything. It had to be obvious to his friends that if Jaden didn't get there until after noon, he'd miss the first game for sure, maybe even the second. That would cut his chances to hit the home run he needed by a quarter, or in half.

"Yeah," Josh said. "I'm fine."

It was a lie. Josh was nowhere close to fine.

CHAPTER SIXTY-SIX

IT TOOK JOSH A long time to get to sleep.

He woke to the clock radio blaring Metallica, and he immediately called Jaden.

"He didn't answer." Jaden sounded worried. "I don't know; did Benji speak to him? Did he get a text or anything?"

Josh had Jaden on speaker phone. Benji looked a little upset, but also a little angry as he shook his head no. "The guy played a professional *game* last night. Jaden, just keep trying. It's not his responsibility to remember; it's ours to remind him."

They agreed that Jaden would just keep trying, and Josh tried to keep his mouth shut even though Benji and his father were driving him absolutely crazy.

They got into their uniforms and headed downstairs

to the hotel dining room for the pregame breakfast buffet.

Coach Swanson acted like nothing had happened. When he saw Josh and Benji, he nodded and said, "Morning, boys."

Benji downed two orders of pancakes with heaps of butter and syrup, and munched on a doughnut while Josh ate a cheese omelet so he'd be ready to play. He was beginning to wonder if he'd dreamed the whole thing until Jack gave him a nasty look from across the dining room. When they got on board the bus, Martin glared at him, as if daring Josh not to give up his cell phone.

When they got to the field, Coach Swanson read off the lineup, putting Noah Canby in for Josh on second. There was a murmur from the team.

Coach looked up from his clipboard and addressed the Titans. "LeBlanc has had a bit of a disciplinary issue. It's between him and me. I don't want anyone discussing it. Hopefully we can get it worked out and get him back in the starting lineup today."

Josh sat on the end of the bench and tried not to look at anyone. It was torture, just sitting there like a lump: no phone, no book, just a prisoner in his own mind. He didn't care about the game, didn't care that they won 7–1 with Esch on the mound. All he could think about was how easily he could have hit a homer off the opposing team's pitcher. He threw nothing but straight, fast pitches without any action on the ball of any kind. When the game ended and they shook hands, Josh realized his jaw hurt from clenching his teeth so hard for so long.

They got back onto the bus, everyone grabbing their phones from Martin's bag. Josh snatched his and returned Martin's dirty look with one of his own. He felt like Martin should feel as bad as anyone and wondered if he could get Coach and the two brothers into any trouble for messing with everyone's phone. Josh sat in the back, and Benji joined him.

"Another big win." Benji had hit a home run of his own during the game, and he happily drummed his fingers on his legs. "Glad I could carry the flag for the heavy hitters."

Josh gave him a blank look, wondering how on earth Benji could think he cared about that game and his home run in the least.

"What?" Benji stared at him. "You disagree?"

"Benji, you were great, but please, call your dad, would you?"

"Well, yeah. Of course I will. I'm sure he's on his way, you know." Benji dialed his phone.

Josh squirmed in his seat, listening to the sound of ringing as it drifted out of Benji's phone. When he heard Benji's father's voice asking people to leave a message, Josh pounded a fist against the bus window.

"Easy, dude," Benji said. "He could be driving. It's

illegal to drive and talk on the phone."

"Your dad doesn't talk when he drives?" Josh spoke through his teeth.

"Sometimes. He could be going past a cop."

Josh shook his head and dialed Jaden. She didn't answer, either. He wanted to smash his phone against the window. He wanted to jump out of the bus. He wanted to melt.

When they got back to the hotel, the team piled into the dining room for lunch. Josh skipped it and headed for his room, leaving Benji with Esch, Lockhart, and Preston.

"Dude," Benji said, "relax. It'll all work out. My dad will be here."

"With Jaden? You said fifty-fifty, Benji." Josh fought to keep his voice down.

"I said fifty-fifty if he'd remember. Jaden will get a hold of him, and he'll bring her. They could walk through that door any minute now. Chill," Benji said.

"I can't 'chill,' Benji. I can't."

Benji shrugged. "Okay, I'm gonna go stoke the furnace. I heard they're serving cheeseburgers. See you in the room."

Josh took the stairs to the second floor and went straight to his room. He threw himself down on the bed and took out his phone. As he did, it rang. He looked at the screen.

It was Jaden.

CHAPTER SIXTY-SEVEN

"WHERE ARE YOU?" JOSH paced the floor.

"Syracuse," she said.

"Why? What happened? When are you coming? Why didn't you call?"

"Josh, I've been trying. I had to go to the hospital to ask my dad. He's working in ICU today, and you can't have cell phones. Mr. Lido isn't leaving until tomorrow morning."

"Jaden, he *can't*." Josh grabbed a handful of his hair and looked at himself in the mirror, a crazed version of the boy he usually knew. "I have to *have* your phone. We *have* to give it to the coach. He said he was coming to see Benji play today. What *happened*?"

"Apparently he hurt himself pretty bad," Jaden said.

"What?" It was too much for Josh, and his voice was

as jagged as a broken bottle. "In the game?"

"No," Jaden said. "The way it sounds, he was playing darts at the Retreat and—I don't know if he fell or what—but he got a dart right through his hand. He freaked and crushed the glass he was holding. Then he fell and drove a piece of the broken glass right into an artery. They had to give him a blood transfusion because he lost so much blood by the time they got it stopped. Anyway, Benji's mom was the one who helped me find all this out. She went over to his apartment. She's pretty mad he's not seeing Benji play, but even she understood that he wanted to take it easy today and leave Sunday morning. He'll still see Benji's last game, and they're still going to the Steelers game. That's what his mom said anyway."

Josh's mouth hung open in disbelief. "I . . . I just can't . . . Unbelievable!"

"Let's look at the bright side," Jaden said.

"Really?" Josh said. "There is one?"

"Well, my dad said I could go; that's one thing. And trust me, that wasn't easy. He couldn't figure out why I had to go to Pittsburgh tomorrow with Mr. Lido and turn right around and come back on the team bus. He wasn't going to let me, but I wouldn't take no for an answer, and finally someone's heart monitor went off and he had to go and he said yes just to get rid of me."

Josh's head was beginning to clear. There was still a possibility. Jaden was right. He had to focus on the chance he had. He had to stay positive. He could do this.

"You're right," he said. "But you *gotta* get here. I *gotta* play in that game tomorrow. It's my last chance."

"We all know that," Jaden said. "Can you hang in there?"

"I have no choice," Josh said. "Do I?"

Jaden got quiet for a moment, then she said, "Unless . . ."

Josh's heart leaped in his chest. "Unless what?"

CHAPTER SIXTY-EIGHT

"**UNLESS COACH SWANSON WILL** trust us," Jaden said. "I could give Mrs. Sheridan my phone. They'd have what they want, and he could let you play later today and all day tomorrow. I'll take the bus to her house. I can be there in less than an hour, maybe half an hour, depending on the bus schedule."

Josh shook his head. "I don't think he'll go for it."

"Shouldn't you try?" she asked.

Josh nodded. "Yes. I will."

Josh didn't waste any time. He went right to the dining room. Coach Swanson was sitting with Coach Moose, who gave Josh a questioning look that told Josh he didn't know what was going on.

"Coach," Josh said to Swanson, "can I talk to you?"

Coach Moose excused himself and got up from the table. Josh sat down.

"I don't see a phone." Coach Swanson studied Josh.

"It's coming," Josh said, "or it was. Jaden needs a ride. Benji's dad was gonna take her, but he got a dart through his hand and . . ."

Josh could see by Coach Swanson's expression that he didn't want to hear any of that.

"What if Jaden gives her phone to Mrs. Sheridan?" Josh asked.

"You tell Jaden to stay away from her." Coach Swanson stabbed his finger at Josh. He leaned forward and lowered his voice. "I said I want that phone. I want it in *my* hands with the pass code, because that's the only way I'll know that file hasn't been sent to anyone. I told you I didn't care how you got it here, and I still don't."

"I need that home run, Coach Swanson." It was all Josh could think of to say.

"If you need a home run, get Jaden and that phone here," he said.

Nothing he could say would change Coach Swanson's mind.

The agony lasted the rest of the day. The team won both games, but Josh sat on the bench. The hardest part might have been when Josh spoke to his own father on the phone. He couldn't say anything about any of it because he didn't know if they could hear what he said on his phone as well as read his texts and also, Josh knew there was nothing his dad could do. It wouldn't be fair to upset him when he had problems of his own.

That night Benji spoke to his dad, who was feeling better and promised he'd set out very early in the morning. Josh tried everything he could think of to convince Benji to talk his dad into leaving that night, but after a while Benji got mad at Josh, and the two of them exchanged some hot words. Josh was so exhausted that he actually went to sleep early.

The next morning, though, he woke at 4:00 a.m. and couldn't get back to sleep.

They had breakfast and Josh ate, forcing himself to think positive. When he got his chance to play, he'd need his strength. The food tasted like glue to him. Benji got defensive when Josh asked him if he had any news.

"Dude, my dad got *hurt*. He could have bled to *death*." Benji scowled. "It's not all about *you* all the time."

Josh bit the inside of his mouth and walked out of the dining room. The team rode to the field on the bus, and although Josh spoke with Jaden during the short trip, Benji's dad still hadn't picked her up by the time he had to turn his phone in before the game. Outside, the sun shone brightly, but inside Josh's head it was a foggy thunderstorm. Josh sat in his same spot on the bench with his skin crawling as the morning game dragged by.

The Titans won again, this time in a last-inning squeaker with Benji hitting a single to knock in the winning run. Benji went wild, and the team swarmed him. Josh stood up from his spot on the bench but didn't join in the group hug. He wasn't a part of it, and no one seemed to care. His teammates all seemed to accept that Coach Swanson had good reason to punish him, and they were evidently emboldened by winning without him. It would have made Josh feel even worse, but he was already at rock bottom.

Even when Coach Swanson gathered the team around him, Josh stayed on the outer edge of the circle.

Coach held up both hands. "Guys, another great win. We get this last one, and it'll be a clean sweep for fall ball. You made me proud, and you did it through hard work and being a team."

"Coach Swanson!"

Everyone turned his head at the sound of a man shouting.

Josh's eyes went from the man rounding the dugout from the stands back to Coach Swanson's look of disbelief.

"Hey, Coach." The man wore a blue Nike sweat suit and track shoes with bright-blue laces. He had dark eyes that matched his dark buzz cut hair and stylish metal-frame glasses that made his serious face even more so. He walked right up to Coach Swanson as if he was the boss.

Josh's heart jumped with excitement at the sight of Ty Rylander, the Nike rep.

CHAPTER SIXTY-NINE

"TY, NICE SURPRISE." COACH Swanson stiffened like the soldier he was, as if awaiting orders.

Josh studied the Nike rep's face, looking for signs of displeasure. His greatest hope was that Ty Rylander was there to chastise the coach for not letting Josh play. His hope flared that Rylander would insist that Josh be put back into the lineup and he could get his twentieth home run. But it fizzled when he saw no such signs.

Instead, Rylander wiggled his nose to shift his glasses into place and smiled. "Well, I've got to be in Chicago tomorrow, and I thought I'd drop in and see if our U13 team can really do what people said couldn't be done: a clean sweep of the YBEL fall ball tournament season. You've done us proud, Coach, and I wanted to take the team to lunch at Primanti Bros. You haven't lived until you've had one of their Almost Famous sandwiches."

Benji stepped up and put a hand on the Nike rep's sleeve. "Mr. Rylander, nothing could be more reward-ing than to celebrate my game-winning RBI with a famous sandwich, or even an almost-famous sandwich. It's like . . . destiny."

The whole team laughed and poked Benji, who grinned from ear to ear. Josh felt even more useless as they piled onto the bus. When he asked Martin where the bag of phones was, Martin frowned at him. "Coach said no phones. He wants the team to bond."

"But—" Josh started to complain, but Martin cut him off with a sharp "No!"

Josh sat by himself in the back of the bus as they cruised into downtown Pittsburgh. Benji was standing in the aisle, walking up and down, slapping high fives and gossiping about what an Almost Famous sandwich could really be. When they got off the bus, Josh was last and surprised to see Benji waiting for him.

"Come on, dude." Benji slung his arm around Josh's shoulder. "You gotta enjoy the moment. Our team is rocking it, and *I* knocked in the winning run. Dude, when you get the win, that's a special moment."

Josh opened his mouth to say something harsh, then exhaled slowly. "Benji, you're right. Sorry, buddy. I should be happy for you, and I am. It's just . . . I thought maybe Jaden figured out a way to get Ty Rylander to come and save the day or something, but he looks like he's ready to give Coach Swanson a contract extension and a raise, and we can't even use our phones to find out where they are."

"Hey, my dad will come through." Benji held up a fist and looked down the city street as if expecting to see his dad's pickup truck at any moment. A bus rounded the corner. Benji shrugged. "Let's go get a sandwich. A man's gotta eat, right?"

"Yeah," Josh said. "I guess."

They walked into the noisy restaurant, packed with people. Ty Rylander apparently knew the owners, because they had pushed several tables together to seat the entire group. Benji and Josh sat on the end farthest from the coaches, the Sheridan brothers, and the Nike rep. As Benji questioned the waitress about what kind of double-meat sandwich was the most popular, Josh couldn't help imagining walking up to Ty Rylander and just telling him everything and begging him to make Coach Swanson let him play in the final game. He was tired and worried and frazzled, and didn't know if he got the chance now whether he even *could* hit the home run he needed.

He ordered an Almost Famous pastrami like Benji just to get the waitress to move on and sat back, pinning everything on the hope that Jaden and Mr. Lido would arrive in time.

When the sandwiches arrived, they were impressed. Soft Italian bread piled high with meat, coleslaw, and

French fries, of all things. Benji got so happy with the flavor of fries and meat and coleslaw, and so intense about eating, he broke out in a sweat.

When he'd finished, Benji looked at Josh's plate like a half-starved dog. "Not hungry?"

Josh sighed and shook his head. He'd taken just two bites.

"You mind?" Benji leaned toward the sandwich.

"It's more pastrami," Josh said.

"Works for me. Hate to see something this pretty go to waste." Benji dug in with both hands.

The meal took longer than Josh liked, and Coach Swanson announced they'd head right for the ballpark instead of go back to the hotel. "Let's win this thing, Titans!"

With a cheer, they boarded the bus and returned to the stadium to face a team from Barbourville, Kentucky, in the championship game. When Josh got off, he went straight to Coach Swanson.

"Coach, can't you let me use my phone? I think Jaden is almost here," he said.

Coach Swanson studied him, then reached into his pocket. "Here, use my phone."

Josh looked at Coach Swanson suspiciously but took it and dialed.

"Hello?" Jaden sounded confused and uncertain.

"Jaden?" Josh could barely breathe. "Where are you?"

CHAPTER SEVENTY

WHEN JOSH GOT OFF the phone, he handed it to Coach Swanson and started to beg. "Coach, please. She's on her way, but they were taking a shortcut on Route 219 and some bridge was closed so they had to go back, and I don't know if they'll make it before the game begins. Jaden didn't share that audio file with anyone. She's sorry. She wants to get here and apologize."

Coach Swanson broke in with an angry voice. "You think you can change my mind?"

"Coach, I—"

Coach Swanson cut him off again. "Look, Josh. I want her to get here. I want to know that she knows she's crossed the line. She's broken a trust. I want that phone, and I want that audio file. When I say something, I mean it. It's the way I am, always was, always will be. She makes it here, you get your shot at the derby. She doesn't, you're finished."

Josh's voice trembled. He was scared and crushed, but he had to go on. "Coach, please. You gotta let me play. I can win that house. My mom and my little sister, we live in Bricktown."

Coach Swanson snorted. "I've seen places that make Bricktown look like New York City's Park Avenue. You'll get through it."

Coach Swanson turned and walked out onto the field without looking back.

CHAPTER SEVENTY-ONE

JOSH SAT IN THE corner of the dugout, depressed and nearly destroyed, watching Canby at second base.

When he felt a hand on his shoulder from behind, he jumped and turned to see Ty Rylander. So many things went through Josh's mind: strategies he could use, markers he could call in using his father's name. Instead, he choked.

"You okay?" Rylander asked.

Josh half nodded, half shook his head.

"Good." Rylander kept his hand on Josh's shoulder but looked out at the field. "Sorry fall ball has to end for you like this, not playing and all, but you know the best coaches I've seen were the toughest ones. I remember when I first started in this business. I was with Adidas, and I got to meet Lou Holtz at Notre Dame. What a battle-ax. He was running his team into the dirt. They were dropping like flies, and he just kept blowing that whistle. It was brutal, and I didn't mean to say anything, but I was like, 'Wow,' and he must have heard me, and you know what he said?"

Josh looked up, but Rylander was still staring out at the field, squinty eyed and dreaming of the past.

"He said, 'Ty, no one has ever drowned in sweat.' How about that? I mean, I know he's known for that quote, but he said it to *me*."

Josh wanted to point out that Holtz was a football coach and this was a baseball team, but instead he said, "Wow."

"Yeah. 'Wow' is right. I don't know what it is you did that caused Coach Swanson to sit you; but he's the coach, and he's gotta be able to make those decisions, even for the best player on the team. You'll be better for all this come spring. The whole team will." Rylander clapped Josh on his shoulder before walking out of the dugout and disappearing in the direction of the stands.

CHAPTER SEVENTY-TWO

IT WAS A 2-2 game in the bottom of the fourth inning when Jaden appeared looking scared and frantic. She slipped into the dugout with her head down, sat next to Josh, removed the phone from her pocket, and placed it in his hand.

"I'm so sorry. Here. The code is 9-8-9-9."

If Coach Swanson noticed Jaden, he didn't show it. He kept focused on the field, where Esch was atop the mound with a 1–2 count on the Barbourville batter. They both knew not to disturb him.

Jaden looked like she was about to cry. "I'm so sorry about this," she said, turning to Josh.

Josh shook his head and touched her arm. "Don't. You're the best friend anyone could ever have."

"Thirty minutes down the thruway, he wanted to

303

stop for *lunch.*" Jaden tried to control her voice. "I was, like, 'Mr. Lido, *please.*' He wasn't happy with me."

Mercifully, Esch struck out his batter, ending the fourth inning.

"Well," Josh said, taking a deep breath, "here goes."

He took the phone over to Coach and told him the password. Coach Swanson grabbed the phone with a stern look and gave it to Martin, who headed out of the dugout like he'd known his orders in advance.

"Coach, can you put me into the lineup now?" Josh begged.

"When Martin says we're good." Coach Swanson's voice was hard, and he walked away, leaving Josh standing in the middle of the dugout as the team filed in.

Josh walked back into the corner where Jaden sat, miserable.

She looked up at him. "Well?"

"I don't know. I guess Martin's going to check to see that you didn't share the file. Can he do that?"

Jaden nodded. "Sure. Everything leaves a footprint if you have the software to track it."

"And . . ." Josh felt guilty asking, but he had to. "He's not going to find anything, right?"

Jaden gave him a weary smile. "No, Josh. We're all set."

"I figured. It's just, you know. You being a devious girl and all that." Josh nudged her.

"Ha ha," she said. "Speaking of devious, hi, Benji."

Josh turned and saw Benji standing there. "Jaden, my dad is here?"

"In the stands with a hot dog in his good hand and a plate of nachos at his feet," Jaden said.

"Man, I'm hungry myself." Benji licked his lips. "Hungry for another shot at this pitcher too. Josh, you ready, dude? I know I struck out in the second, but we can hit this guy. I was worried about facing Tucker Holland. Everyone's talking about the no-hitter he threw in his last tournament. I don't know why he's not pitching, but *this* kid's a heavy hitter's dream—high and hot, that's all he's got."

"I still need Coach to give me the okay." Josh had barely paid attention to the pitcher, but even as distracted as he'd been, he knew Benji was right. The pitcher guy was a home run waiting to be hit.

Esch cracked a ball into the left-center gap and stopped at second, bouncing on the bag, grinning, and exchanging a thumbs-up with Coach Moose, who shouted with both hands around his mouth. "Atta boy, Esch!"

Instead of feeling better, Josh felt worse. He kept glancing at the door in the back of the dugout. He knew there was Wi-Fi in the brick clubhouse connected to the dugout by a tunnel; he assumed that's where Martin had gone.

Goldie struck out before Jack Sheridan stepped up to the plate. Jack banged one deep into left field. Josh willed it over the fence because a home run would give them a 4–2 lead, and he felt like a happy Coach Swanson would be good for him. The left fielder leaped, made the catch before he hit the wall, and fell into a heap. Esch tagged up and took off from second base. Josh held his breath as the outfielder got up slowly, reared back, and fired a bullet just as Esch rounded third with Coach Moose waving him on.

The shortstop cut off the throw, turned, and fired it to the catcher, low and hard so that it cracked when the ball hit his glove. Esch slid with perfect form, and it looked like a tie as a cloud of dust exploded above the plate.

The umpire leaned in and yanked out his thumb. "Yer out!"

The abrupt end of the inning filled Josh with panic. He darted toward the back door to the dugout, praying for Martin to return, knowing he had to get into the lineup at the bottom of the inning if he was to have a chance to bat in the next.

He gripped the handle and flung the door wide.

CHAPTER SEVENTY-THREE

JOSH SAW NOTHING BUT an empty underground hallway leading under the stands into the clubhouse. He glanced back over his shoulder. Players were grabbing their gloves and heading out onto the field. Esch started to the mound, still dusting himself off.

Josh looked back, and his heart gushed with joy as Martin appeared, heading his way. Josh looked back into the dugout. "Coach, he's here! Coach!"

Coach Swanson walked over with his arms folded across his chest. He barked out into the hallway. "Martin! Thumbs up or thumbs down?"

Martin's thumb was sideways. Josh wanted to scream.

"Thumbs up," Martin called. "It's all good!"

Hope and fear crowding his mind, Josh turned to the coach.

"Okay, LeBlanc, take second," Coach Swanson said. He got Canby's attention and waved him in before Josh made it out of the dugout.

CHAPTER SEVENTY-FOUR

THE SUN WAS LOW in the sky, nestling down into a bed of purple clouds pushing in from the west. The stadium lights hummed and glowed white with hints of blue and green. Josh caught a whiff of grass and hot popcorn, and his heart galloped inside his chest as he took his position near second base. Josh made a few extra pegs to first as Coach gave the home plate umpire the lineup switch.

Before he knew it, the first batter was up. Josh pounded his glove and got ready. Esch sat the batter down with four pitches.

The next batter let a strike go by, then blasted a line drive right at Josh. It was so hot he barely knocked it down. Josh didn't miss a beat, though; he scooped up the ball and rifled it to first, throwing the runner out on a close call. His teammates cheered.

Josh took a deep breath of the cool evening air and laughed out loud.

Baseball was a beautiful thing.

Esch struck out the third batter, and the Titans jogged quickly back to the dugout, inspired by their pitcher and the momentum he'd created. Josh knew he'd get only one chance to bat. Since he replaced Canby, he'd be batting right after Benji.

Jaden sat in the corner of the dugout, still looking uncomfortable. "I feel so weird sitting here. Martin and Coach act like I don't exist."

Josh sat next to her and whispered, "Everything will be okay."

"Will it?" she asked.

"I think so, yeah. I think as long as that story doesn't get written, Coach Swanson's okay. He shut it down, and he's moving on."

"I just don't understand why Coach and Martin were so upset. It's a great story, with Swanson as the hero." Jaden shook her head. "I hope Martin can forgive me."

"Coach is a really private person. I guess he didn't want his private life made public. And you can get back with Martin. I'm sure you will. Just be honest with him and tell him why you wanted to write the story."

Grabbing his batting helmet, Benji bumped fists with Jaden. "You and my old man saving the day, huh?"

"I'm glad we made it," Jaden said.

Jaden watched Benji hurrying to the on-deck circle. "I started another story, you know."

"Really?" Josh said. "What's it about?"

Jaden looked at him. "You."

"Me?"

"The whole Home Run Derby thing," she said. "I mean, if you qualify, it's a super story: you coming back from Florida to try and win your mom a house; it's very gallant. Like a knight."

Josh heard a couple of his teammates groan in unison, and he turned his attention to the field, where a new pitcher was taking the mound for Barbourville.

"What just happened?" Jaden asked.

Josh stared at the new kid climbing the mound. "For this story, the Dark Lord of Mordor has arrived."

CHAPTER SEVENTY-FIVE

JADEN BLINKED. *"THAT'S* THEIR ace pitcher, Tucker Holland?"

"You heard of him, right?" Josh had come to automatically rely on Jaden to scout their opponents.

"Sure," she said. "I thought we— Well, we would have talked about it if I'd been here. He's the top pitcher in the tournament, but I thought he'd be bigger than that."

"He's not small," Josh said.

"No, but they clocked his fastball at eighty-one miles an hour," she said. "And he throws a lot more than a fastball."

"Great," Josh said. "Just what I needed. The best pitcher around and maybe only one shot at a home run."

"Hopefully you'll get that homer." Jaden's lip

disappeared beneath a row of perfect white front teeth.

"Hopefully?" Josh was almost too worn down to get excited.

"Well," she said. "You heard Benji talk about his no-hitter. Some days he mixes in a slider with his fastball, but I know his out pitch is a twelve-to-six curve."

They sat without speaking as Tucker Holland struck out first Goldie, then Jack Sheridan with ease. With Benji up, Josh was on deck.

It was time. Josh stood up. Jaden stood up too.

She hugged him and kissed his cheek before he could think. "That house will be yours, Josh."

Josh nervously polished his batting helmet on his leg, pretending his cheeks weren't hot from the kiss. "Let's hope you're right."

CHAPTER SEVENTY-SIX

COACH SWANSON WALKED OUT of the dugout to talk with Benji. He leaned into him with both arms resting on Benji's shoulders. "C'mon, Benji. You won the last one for us. I know I've been hard on you all season, but it's paid off. You can do this."

Benji laughed and winked at the coach like some kind of pirate ready to board a ship laden with gold. "You know me, Coach; I'm a heavy hitter. Always have been, always will be."

Coach Swanson stiffened and shook his head. "Yeah, Benji. But now all I want from you is a single. Just get on base. This Holland kid's got more tricks than a Las Vegas magician. Can you get me a hit?"

"Consider it done, Coach." Benji gave the coach a nod

and marched toward the plate, giving the Barbourville pitcher his best evil eye.

If Tucker Holland was impressed, he didn't show it. He read the catcher's signal, shook it off, then nodded at the next signal, wound up, and fired a curveball. Benji swung so hard, he corkscrewed into the dirt. Laughter sprinkled down onto the field from the stands, but one voice rang out.

Mr. Lido was on his feet and red faced. "Go get yourself one, Benji! Swing for the fences and win this thing!"

Josh was suddenly filled with a new kind of panic. He hadn't even thought of what happened if Benji hit a home run; but if he did, the Titans would win 3–2, and the game would be over.

"Benji!" His friend's name burst from Josh's lips. "Benji! Remember what Coach said!"

Coach Swanson stood outside the dugout with his arms folded across his chest. He reinforced Josh's plea with a curt nod. "Benji. A *hit*. Get me a hit. That is all we need."

Something in Benji's face told Josh that he wasn't listening to the coach. He knew that Mr. Lido had absolute power over Benji's mind, and there was nothing Josh could do about it.

The pitch came in, a fastball right down the middle, something Josh dreamed of getting. Benji swung for the fences. The bat cracked, and the ball flew.

Benji took off down the first-base line, watching the left fielder backpedal for all he was worth. The ball began to drop. Benji rounded first, heading for second, pumping both fists up over his head like a true champion.

The ball was gone.

CHAPTER SEVENTY-SEVEN

MAYBE IT WAS THE breath of God or maybe just a cold front blowing in from Ohio.

Either way, Josh felt the blast of cold air and knew that it saved his chance at the Home Run Derby. Benji's ball fell just short of the wall. The left fielder played the bounce perfectly, turned back toward the infield, and fired to third in one continuous motion. Benji was fifteen feet off third and pulled up short, racing back to second.

The third baseman threw to the second baseman, who snatched it and quick as a blink tagged Benji. The umpire was right there, bent over and watching, and Josh felt it all slip away until the umpire stood straight and slashed his arms. "Safe!"

Relief poured through Josh only to ebb and give way to a flood of worry.

This was the chance he'd been praying for the past two days. Now it was up to him. He had to do it. He had to get his twentieth home run. It would not only win the game, it would send him to Houston the very next weekend for his appointment with destiny.

It had to be his destiny, didn't it?

Josh walked to the plate, breathing deep and working out the kinks in his neck. He thought about Florida, his dad, and the team he'd left there. It seemed like another lifetime. His arms felt sluggish, and he shook them out, one at a time, swapping the bat from hand to hand. The wind was stiff in his face, working against him, but he pushed that from his mind, took one final big breath, rounded the plate, and stepped into the box.

"Josh!" Coach Swanson yelled through a cup made from both of his iron hands.

Josh's jaw went slack. He stepped out.

"Left side, Josh." Coach Swanson wasn't asking. "Take away that slider."

It was a good call, and Josh warmed to his coach because it was something his dad would have thought of, and something Josh should have. The impact on Tucker Holland was obvious. When Josh circled to the other side of the plate, his face fell.

"Heavy hitter! Heavy hitter!" Benji howled from second base.

Josh bit his lip, took a swing, and stepped up to the plate.

He saw the slider and swung for everything he was worth.

SMACK!

He pulled it way inside the first-base line, but the ball flew past the pole and out of the park. The crowd behind him buzzed with excitement. His teammates stood frozen in the anticipation of a game winner gone foul. Jaden clenched both hands on either side of her face.

"You got this, heavy hitter!" Benji yelled. "You got this. Destiny! It's all about the heavy hitters!"

Josh stepped back. The wind shrieked through the ear holes in his helmet. Holland wound up and threw. Fastball. Low and inside, and Josh wasn't buying it.

"Strike!" The umpire yelled so loud it hurt Josh's ears.

The crowd murmured.

Coach Swanson lost his mind. "That's awful! That's horrible! That's the worst call I've seen in my *life!*"

Josh breathed deep and pushed it out of his mind. It was an 0–2 count with everything against him: the pitcher, the wind, and now even the umpire. He could either dig in or go home. He could crumble or stand. He could win or lose.

He gripped the bat and heard his father's voice.

"Treat every pitch the same. You have to look at a

0–2 count at the bottom of the sixth with two outs the same as the first pitch of the day. That's what the great ones do. Derek Jeter could strike out three times in a row but always went back to the dugout saying, 'He's not that good. I can hit him. You guys can hit him.'"

How many times had he heard his father say that?

Josh knew it was true. He also knew that when a pitcher felt in control, he went to his out pitch. Holland's out pitch, according to Jaden, was the slow twelve-to-six curveball. Like Clayton Kershaw's. The only way to hit it is see the spin, let it drop, and follow it to the bottom of the strike zone before you swing. Josh stepped into the box, glad to be on the left-hand side.

Holland wound up and threw. The ball's rotation screamed curveball.

Josh waited, knowing he could go down and get it.

He thought about that house.

He thought about his mom and Laurel.

He swung the bat.

CHAPTER SEVENTY-EIGHT

JOSH SWUNG SO HARD at the falling pitch that the tip of the bat touched the back of his heel. It was gone. Even Tucker Holland watched it go.

Joy and relief and gratitude overran Josh's brain. It was as if that strong wind lifted him from his feet to dance like a kite as he rounded the bases and came home to a sloppy kiss from Benji and a swarm of cheering Titans.

It all blended together: the laughter and the trophies, the applause and the handshakes, the smiles and the hugs. And then they were quiet and riding up the thruway. The bus swayed like a cradle, rocking the players to sleep, but Josh sat rigid in the backseat with Jaden next to him, typing intently on her computer, her face aglow.

Jaden stopped typing and looked up at him. "I'm surprised you're not asleep. You look wiped out."

"Just thinking," he said. "How's the article?"

"I wish I had another week," she said, "but I heard Diana Henriques wrote her story about American soldiers in a day."

"And Diana Henriques would be?"

"The 2005 Pulitzer Prize–winning writer for the *New York Times.*" Jaden looked at him like he didn't know who Mike Trout was. "Actually, she was the finalist for the prize. She had all the background, but I've got to dig for mine. I'll call the company tomorrow and find out who thought of the contest, how long it's been running, how many winners they've had. That sort of thing."

"Well, that's good then." He sighed. "There's only one thing that would make me happier than you winning your journalist contest and that scholarship."

"Winning your mom a house," she said. "I know. Can you imagine the impact of the story if you really *won*?"

Josh stared at her. In front of them, one of Josh's teammates snored.

"You don't think I can win it, do you," he said.

"Well, don't say that," she said. "I . . . Josh, it'll be very hard. It's a bathtub you're swinging for, not the fences. I love that you're trying, and I love that you made it this far, but . . ."

"I know," he said. "It's okay. But maybe."

"Maybe," she said. "For sure."

Josh rested his head against the window and fell asleep hoping to dream about what just might happen.

CHAPTER SEVENTY-NINE

THE FOLLOWING SATURDAY, THE last weekend in October, Jaden's dad took them to the airport and escorted them onto the plane before departing for the hospital. Qwik-E-Builders gave the derby finalists a plane ticket for themselves and one guest. Josh gave his extra ticket to Benji since Jaden was being flown down to Houston by the newspaper. Bud Poliquin, the editor she'd worked with before, was betting her story about Josh's quest would be award winning. He planned to publish it on Monday, November first.

They made their connection in Atlanta, with Jaden navigating the enormous airport like a professional traveler. Josh's dad picked them up at the Houston airport, looking leaner and with tanner skin than Josh ever remembered him having.

Josh shook his father's hand. "Hi, Dad."

"Come here, you." His father pulled him into a bear hug that took Josh's breath away, then his father held him at arm's length. "Look at you. You look good. Taller too."

Josh's dad greeted his friends, then took them all to the Omni hotel downtown. After checking in, they went out to the Astros baseball complex hosting the derby. He knew there were thirteen finalists from around the country, and he saw four of them in the shuttle van on the way out to the field.

While the winner of the derby who hit the most home runs got a five-thousand-dollar scholarship, the red bathtub just beyond the center-field fence, propped up at an angle for all to see, was all Josh could think about.

An official who wore a dark-blue blazer with a Qwik-E-Builders Home Run Derby name tag explained the rules of the practice round. "Once you start, you'll get a pitch from the machine every fifteen seconds, four a minute for five minutes. Good luck today and in the main event tomorrow."

Benji and Jaden watched from the seats behind home plate while Josh's dad went with Josh out onto the field. A kid named Dale Schwamman from Turkey Valley, Iowa, banged every other pitch over the fence before Josh got his chance.

When Josh finally dug in, he hit a line drive on the

first pitch that bounced off the machine.

His father laughed. "Okay, you'll get it. Don't try and dip under it. You just have to get used to the machine."

The next pitch Josh hit deep into right field, then he put one over on the third pitch. The fourth went over the wall as well, both center right, a good ways away from the bathtub. He huffed in frustration.

"Relax," his dad said.

Josh tried. The fifth hit went to deep left field. He kept hitting and drove seven of his twenty over the fence. The seventeenth bounced six feet from the bathtub, causing Benji and Jaden to scream as it dropped. The next three were closer, but none even dinged the tub.

"Better you didn't waste it on the practice round." Josh's father clapped a big hand on Josh's neck as they walked off the field toward the stairway leading into the stands.

Josh shook from exertion and nerves.

That night they ate at Brennan's, a fancy old place that served Creole food more common to New Orleans. Benji ordered a second bread pudding and declared it the dessert he knew he'd be eating in heaven one day.

"What makes you think you're headed up and not down?" Jaden asked with a mischievous smile.

Benji didn't miss a beat. "Anyone who's kind and patient enough to be friends with a grump like you gets an automatic spot in heaven."

He showed his pleasure by stuffing a spoonful of pudding into his mouth that was big enough to leave whipped cream skid marks on his cheeks.

Later that night Josh had trouble getting to sleep. His father snored in the bed next to his. Jaden and Benji each had beds in the connecting room. Josh got up and softly opened the door to their room. Benji had his mouth wide open and his eyes closed in a peaceful sleep. Jaden sat propped up on pillows typing away. He knew she was excited about her interviews with the Quik-E-Builders people.

She looked up at him and blinked. "All I need now is the happy ending. You ready?"

Josh sat down on the edge of her bed and kept his voice low. "Yes and no. How can you ever be ready for something like this? But I'm as ready as I'll ever be. . . ."

Jaden covered his hand with her own and gave it a squeeze. "Even if you don't, it's a sensational story. Not every quest ends with the Holy Grail."

She paused and seemed uncertain about what she was going to say next.

Josh felt his muscles tighten.

Jaden shook her head as if ridding herself from all thoughts.

"You should sleep the sleep of a hero," she said. "You've done everything you can think of to help your family."

"I wish he'd do everything he could to help our

family." Josh nodded his head toward the room where his father slept. "That stupid Diane."

Jaden sighed. "He's here. He loves you a lot, Josh. That's more than a lot of kids can say."

"Really?" he asked, squinting at her.

"Really," she said.

Josh thought about that, then in a whisper he said, "I gotta win this thing."

Jaden whispered back. "You might. I keep saying that."

He looked right at her. "I think it's my destiny. I really do."

The next morning Josh didn't want to talk to anyone. It was game day times a million to him. He was concentrating. He was visualizing that ball and that big red bathtub he planned to drop it into. They boarded the bus, and all thirteen contestants and their guests rumbled out to the field. They changed into their respective uniforms in the visitor's clubhouse. They drew numbered balls from a bag to determine the order. Josh reached into the felt sack, got hold of one ball, but switched it for another at the last second and pulled out thirteen.

Dale, the kid from Iowa, looked at Josh's number. "Last, that's lucky."

Someone behind them barked with laughter. "Lucky? Thirteen is as unlucky as you can get."

Josh never figured out who said that, but he couldn't

stop thinking about it as they marched out onto the field in a small parade. The stands weren't full, but the TV cameras for ESPN 3 added plenty of excitement.

The Qwik-E-Builders president, a man named Bert Bell, gave a speech about excellence in baseball and home building, comparing the two. "Finally, while the winner who hits the most balls over the fence will receive a five-thousand-dollar college scholarship, the prize we're all here for is a U-Built-It three-bedroom Streamline Ranch. Any player who hits a homer into the big red bathtub you can all see resting just beyond the center-field fence and that ball *stays* in the tub wins a free Streamline Ranch home for his family. The Streamline Ranch is the model we at Qwik-E-Builders call America's Dream. Good luck, boys."

Everyone clapped politely, and the derby began.

Josh sat in the dugout, watching and waiting. He couldn't see his friends and father from where he sat, and he'd never felt more alone in his life. The warm air and sunshine seemed to choke him. He began to sweat. Three boys hit balls that came close enough to the bathtub to draw cheers from the crowd, but each one dropped just to the side or behind the tub. Dale from Iowa hit eleven home runs, but none of them even close to the tub. Josh began to think about Jaden's words when they first talked about the derby at the end of the summer. She called it a scam, and Josh couldn't help but wonder if that's what it was.

It took forever, but finally Josh's turn came.

He stepped up to the plate and could pick out Benji, Jaden, and his dad cheering from the seats behind the backstop. Josh took a deep breath and stepped into the box.

He gave the official a nod. The official nodded back, pressed a button on the remote in his hands, and the machine starting pitching.

CHAPTER EIGHTY

JOSH BANGED THE FIRST pitch hard. It rose up and up, on a beeline for center field and the bathtub. It was too good to be true, that's all Josh could think. Like a hole in one. As it dropped toward the tub, right at it, Josh blinked and knew he needed to get ready for his next pitch, but he couldn't. This was it. This was his destiny.

CHAPTER EIGHTY-ONE

HIS HOMER WENT BEYOND the tub, just beyond it.

The crowd groaned and so did Josh. The next pitch came at him. He barely got a piece of it. His rhythm was off. He tried to focus. His next eight hits fell short of the fence, scattered across the field like he was some marginal batter, not a home run champion. His ninth hit went over the left-field fence, proving he'd gotten his groove back. The crowd cheered for him and so did the other players in the dugout, rooting and hoping he'd get that house. The five-thousand-dollar scholarship was already out of reach. Dale still held the lead with eleven home runs, and there was no way Josh could catch him. Still, he could win that house.

Josh's next hit went straight to center field but landed short of the tub. The next three went over the fence, home runs, but off to either side before he hit three wild ones. He had three pitches left. Three. Three chances to rescue his mom and his little sister. He *had* to do it. He could do it. He *would* do it.

He felt suddenly calm.

Destiny.

The word filled his mind and his body too.

The pitch came. He banged it. Center field, over the fence. Just to the right.

Two pitches left, but he was cool.

Bang.

Center field, but just to the left.

There was a groove he had to hit between the two. The crowd went wild. The pitch came in.

Crack!

The ball flew up and away, dead bang in the middle of the field with just the right distance.

Josh couldn't even breathe. He dropped his bat and watched the ball fall straight for the big red tub in the middle of his dream.

CHAPTER EIGHTY-TWO

BANG!

The ball struck the tub's bottom.

Clangbangthump!

It rebounded off the side, the bottom, the other side . . . and out of the tub.

The crowd went silent. Josh went numb. Bert Bell, the Qwik-E-Builders president, was coming toward him with a handheld microphone and a big grin. He clapped Josh on the back and spoke to the crowd. "Ladies and gentlemen, let's give Josh LeBlanc a big big big Qwik-E-Builders round of applause. He was *so* close!"

The applause was weak and dribbled into a disappointed murmur.

Bert Bell cleared his throat. "Ladies and gentlemen, let's now hear it for our 2016 Qwik-E-Builders Home

Run Derby champion and the winner of a *five-thousand-dollar* college scholarship . . . Dale Schwamman from Iowa!"

Josh didn't hear the applause or feel the handshakes of the other kids. He didn't taste the lunch they ate on their way to the airport, didn't feel his father's good-bye hug or even the turbulence that turned Benji green as they flew into Syracuse in the heart of a thunderstorm. Jaden sat next to him, equally distracted by her computer, which she attacked like a ninja.

Josh was numb.

His mother met him at the door, greeting him with a kiss and a big hug. "Oh, Josh. You were so close. I am *so* proud."

He let himself be kissed and hugged by Laurel before excusing himself. In his bedroom with the door shut, Josh lay down and stared at the ceiling. Through the walls, he could hear their next-door neighbors shouting at each other. There was a loud bang then quiet before Josh thought he could just make out the low hum of sobbing.

And then everything that had happened in the last few weeks came crashing down on him. From his father's move to Florida, to Benji thinking Jack was older than thirteen, to almost missing his twentieth home run because of Jaden's story about the coach, and now this. It was all just too much. Josh turned and buried his face in the pillow and lost it completely.

CHAPTER EIGHTY-THREE

MONDAY HE WOKE EARLY. His mom sat at the kitchen table with a cup of coffee, reading the online version of the Syracuse paper on her computer.

She glanced up at him. "You should take a look at this. That Jaden, I can't believe she's thirteen. She's something."

"Yeah." Josh took a box of cereal from the cupboard and poured the cereal into a bowl before dousing it with milk. "She is."

"Don't you want to see it?" his mother asked.

Josh shoveled in a mouthful of Raisin Bran and shook his head. "Not really."

"It's about *you*." His mom spun her computer around so he could see.

Josh looked down at his bowl and poked at a raisin

while he crunched. "There's only so many nice ways you can candy coat a loser."

"The way she describes it, you're no loser, Josh. She's calling for an investigation of the whole contest. Jaden's got a quote from the marketing guy at the company you wouldn't believe. She's got statistics on the number of kids who've tried and failed. You should see the comments coming in. This thing is red-hot. People are mad. There's a guy whose brother is in Houston, where Qwik-E-Builders headquarters is, who's talking about a boycott."

Josh sighed. "Jaden has to mind her own business. Looking into things almost got me thrown out of the tournament. It just causes trouble. And none of it is gonna do us much good, is it?"

"I . . . I don't know, Josh."

"It's not, Mom. They're a multimillion-dollar corporation, and I'm a nobody who came up short, and that's putting it nicely." Josh suddenly wasn't hungry. He dumped his cereal in the sink, rinsed his bowl, and closed himself off in his room to get ready for school.

When Josh shut his locker at the end of the day, Benji was standing there. "Dude, this is big and getting bigger. They're calling that company Tricky Quickie Builders. My brother texted me. This thing is going viral, dude. Someone posted a video of your home run bouncing out of the tub. People are saying it's impossible to have a ball hit that far *stay* in the tub. Some people are saying *Mythbusters* is gonna do a show on it."

"Yeah, I'll believe that when I see it." Josh slung his backpack over his shoulder and headed for the bus.

Benji hustled to keep up. "Dude, you're practically famous, and you're moping around like you lost the World Series or something."

Tuesday was long, and Josh was in no mood for everyone's sad eyes and sympathy. The claps on his back and the indignant remarks about Qwik-E-Builders did nothing to help his mood. He struggled to remain polite and avoided Jaden as much as he could because all everyone else wanted to talk about with her was her firebomb online story or column or whatever the heck it was.

Even Benji couldn't snap him out of his funk. When Jaden asked him on the bus why he was mad at her, his face softened for the first time in days. "I'm not, Jaden. I just want this to end. I know you didn't mean anything by it, but that thing you wrote and people who don't even know me making a bunch of noise. It's just . . . embarrassing is what it is."

"Well," she said. "I'm sorry for that, Josh. But the derby was a scam. You and a lot of other kids were tricked. The marketing guy even said it would take a miracle to have a ball stay in the tub. I'm glad people are getting mad about it and demanding action. That's why I want to be a reporter."

"Hey," Josh said, brightening. "I bet with all this hoopla you'll win that scholarship!"

"Maybe," Jaden said.

"I think you will."

On Wednesday at school Jaden and Benji both acted weird to Josh, but they gave him his space and that was the thing he wanted most, so no big deal.

When he got home, his mom gave him this funny look, and she had on some nice clothes.

"You got a job interview?" he asked.

"Yeah . . . well, not really." She was busy in the kitchen, and Josh didn't have time for double talk.

He retreated to his room, sat down at his desk, and started in on his homework. Maybe a half hour went by before he heard a knock. "Laurel, I'll play with you in a couple minutes. Let me finish these math problems. You get the board set up, and I'll be out there."

"No, Josh. It's me," his mother said.

"What, Mom?"

"I need you to come out here."

Josh opened the door and saw that she had on her coat, with Laurel riding on her hip.

"Come on." She started toward the door. "Get your coat. I've got a surprise for you."

Josh was annoyed. "Mom, I've got math homework to do."

"Come on, Josh. Please." She made her eyes so big he couldn't refuse.

"Where are we going?" His voice was sullen, but when he stepped out onto the front step with her, he saw the long, black limousine.

"Mom? What is that?"

CHAPTER EIGHTY-FOUR

THE LONG CAR'S DOOR swung open. Benji's and Jaden's faces appeared, and his friends motioned for him to join them.

"Come on, dude!" Benji hollered. "I bet you were late for your own birthday, I swear."

Josh looked at his mom. She started to laugh, a bubbly laugh he hadn't heard in ages. "Go on, Josh. It's something good."

Josh was confused. "I don't want everyone trying to make me feel good, Mom. This is a waste of money. I hope nobody had to pay for this thing."

"Just get in, Grouchy Pants," she said.

They all got in, but they didn't drive very far. Just off Eighth North Street they pulled down the short road where Josh had seen the lots for sale. He was even more confused when he saw a small crowd of people and several TV trucks sprouting antennae and satellite dishes. The car eased up into the middle of the crowd. Josh got out with his mom and his friends and stepped onto a red carpet.

It was like another dream, but it was real. Everyone was there, his teammates and classmates and everybody's parents too. There was a huge crane parked on the street, its arm reaching over the top of a raised platform atop which stood—among others—Coach Swanson, Coach Moose, Ty Rylander, and Bert Bell, the Qwik-E-Builders president. Bell grinned from ear to ear, and he held out a hand for Josh to shake as Josh mounted the steps leading to the red-carpeted platform. That's when he saw his father near Ty Rylander and darted into his arms, accepting a hug.

"Dad?"

"You think I'd miss this?" His father squeezed him tight before setting him down.

"Miss what? I'm not even sure what is happening!"

The crowd broke out into a little cheer. Jaden, Benji, and Josh's mom and sister stood beside him on the opposite side of his dad. He didn't know what to say, but his heart was pounding like it needed to get out.

"Josh," Bert Bell said, turning from Josh to address the crowd and the cameras up front. "We looked at the rules for the Home Run Derby, and we decided to reevaluate our contest. As your very sharp-tongued friend pointed out—"

Bert Bell paused to nod at Jaden, and everyone laughed.

"We determined that we made a mistake, and that's not what Qwik-E-Builders is all about. And when mistakes happen, good people fix them." Bert Bell handed Josh a big pair of scissors before pointing to a lonesome door standing all by itself on the edge of the platform, a door with a big red ribbon across it. "So please cut this ceremonial ribbon and walk through the door that goes with the brand-new Qwik-E-Builders Streamline Ranch that we will be assembling over the next few days, right here, on this lot we're purchasing for you and your family."

Josh had no idea what else he could do besides cut the ribbon, so he did.

Everyone cheered.

He hugged his mom and his friends all at once, crying, and thanking Jaden and Benji for helping make it all happen.

"Any time," Benji said, chuckling like a madman.

In all the noise and excitement, Jaden turned to him, her yellow-green eyes sparkling with mischief.

"What's next for the heavy hitters?" she asked.

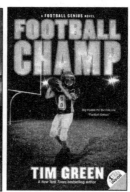

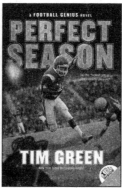

ALSO FROM
TIM GREEN

BE SURE TO CATCH ALL OF THE BASEBALL GREAT NOVELS

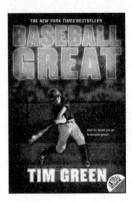 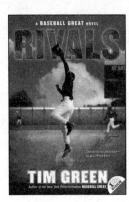 

PLUS TIM GREEN'S OTHER HOME-RUN HITS

 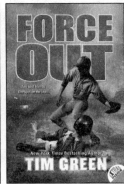  

HARPER
An Imprint of HarperCollinsPublishers

www.timgreenbooks.com